BOOK 3

HIGH SIERRA ADVENTURE

S · E · R · I · E · S

Setting the Trap

Jeff Nesbit

OLIVER
NELSON

THOMAS NELSON PUBLISHERS
Nashville · Atlanta · London · Vancouver

YA
NES

Published in Nashville, Tennessee, by Thomas Nelson, Inc., Publishers, and distributed in Canada by Word Communications, Ltd., Richmond, British Columbia.

Library of Congress Cataloging-in-Publication Data

Nesbit, Jeffrey Asher.
    Setting the trap / Jeff Nesbit.
        p.   cm.—(High Sierra adventure series)
    Summary: Twelve-year-old Josh Landis has a chance to use some of the knowledge he has gained since moving to the High Sierras with his mother and stepfather, a park ranger, when he helps look for the person who has been setting rusty old traps and wounding animals.
    ISBN 0-8407-9256-5 (pbk.)
    [1. Sierra Nevada (Calif. and Nev.)—Fiction.
2. Trapping—Fiction. 3. Stepfathers—Fiction.
4. Christian life—Fiction.] I. Title. II. Series: Nesbit, Jeffrey Asher. High Sierra adventure series.
PZ7.N4378Se   1994
[Fic]—dc20   93-41025
                                                    CIP
                                                    AC

Printed in the United States of America.

    1   2   3   4   5   6 — 99 98 97 96 95 94

To Elizabeth,
who is every bit as courageous
and resourceful as Ashley.

△ CHAPTER 1

△OK, so Ashley was right. Well, not exactly *right*. But close enough.

Ashley—my next-door neighbor and kind of my best friend, even if she is a girl—said that I'd never get my mom to agree to let us go out camping in the wilderness alone. No way, Ashley said. We had to go with a grown-up.

The High Sierras are rugged wilderness once you get beyond the foothills and the small pockets of houses gathered there. Only the rangers and the occasional backpackers or mule trains spend time in the heart of the High Sierras, and mostly in the summer.

Still, I figured it was worth a shot. I was twelve. I'd learned enough to be able to hold my own out in the woods. I was becoming a better animal tracker with each passing day. I could tell the difference between a fox and a regular old dog, for instance.

And I'd been out in the woods so much that I knew my way around. I was even learning how to forage for food, though it was a whole lot easier just to come home at the end of the day and sit down at the dinner table with Mom and my stepfather, Mark, who was a National Park Service ranger.

But, like I said, Ashley was right. Mom just glared at me like I'd lost my mind when I asked her what she thought about the idea of maybe camping out for a couple of days. In a few years, maybe, if I was good, she'd said only half jokingly.

I reminded her that I'd survived our hunt for the old cougar that had been killing sheep. When they'd finally tracked and killed the sheep killer, I'd been right there. And nothing had happened to me.

I hadn't told Mom that, in fact, the old cougar was still out there. Both Ashley and I knew it had been the old gray cougar's offspring that had been killing the sheep. And it had been *that* cougar, the young one, the hunters had finally killed.

The old cougar still lived. It would still outwit hunters by disappearing from trees in the middle of the night or vanishing into the caverns of long-abandoned mineshafts. But of course that was another story.

We were now in the middle of the summer. It had been a couple of months since we'd moved from Washington, D.C., to California, near the High Sierra National Park.

I wasn't so miserable anymore. Ashley was a blast to hang out with. She always wanted to do something, either hike up something or bike over to see this old Indian woman who lived by herself or go swimming at a creek we'd discovered near our two houses.

She was practically at my door when I got up each morning. We'd be sitting there eating breakfast, and we'd hear this soft knock at the back door. Just like this morning.

"Come in, Ashley," my mother called out sweetly.

The door opened slowly. Ashley peeked in. "You sure? Are you finished with breakfast yet?"

It was like half an hour before the roosters woke up. It wasn't even full daylight yet. But Ashley was rip-roaring ready to go. Heaven only knew what she had planned for this day.

"We're just sitting down, honey," Mom told her. "But you're more than welcome to join us."

"Um, well, no, that's OK," Ashley said quickly. "I'll just kind of hang out, then."

"Why don't you hang out at the table with us?" my stepfather, Mark, suggested, chuckling.

I couldn't quite call Mark "Dad" yet. Maybe I'd never be able to. I don't know. My dad had died a few years ago. That was who I thought of when I thought of my father.

Don't get me wrong. Mark is a cool guy. I like him. He does lots of neat stuff, like letting me come by the ranger station to work sometimes. Things like that. But he isn't my father.

Ashley edged into the kitchen. "Yeah, well, I could just grab a chair."

"Why don't you do that," Mom said. "And if you see something you like on the table, help yourself. There's plenty to go around."

Ashley took a chair. I almost cracked up. She did

this just about every morning. She'd get here, pretend like she wouldn't eat anything, and then wind up eating more than me.

My mom sat down. "Some juice?" she asked Ashley.

"Um, well, OK, sure," Ashley said.

"Some eggs, maybe, and a sausage?" Mom asked.

Ashley nodded. She'd already grabbed a biscuit and taken a huge bite, so she couldn't actually answer. Mom heaped some eggs and a sausage on her plate. Ashley dug in.

It was weird, actually. Ashley ate like crazy, but she was skinnier than I was. I think it was because she went through the day like a tornado. She never stopped for anything. She went from one thing to the next like the world would end if she didn't do everything as fast as possible.

"So what are you guys doing today?" asked Mark.

"I dunno," I mumbled. I really wasn't completely awake yet. I didn't know how Ashley was so wide awake. What did she do, get up and practice or something?

"I think I found a mink den!" Ashley said between bites.

"No way," I said, incredulous. "Really?"

Mark frowned. "Are you sure? I didn't think minks came down this far south in the Sierras."

"Beats me if they do or they don't," Ashley answered. "All I know is that I'm pretty sure it's a mink."

"How do you know?" I demanded.

Ashley frowned at me. "The tracks, silly."

"Where'd you see them?" I asked.

"Down near the creek the other day."

"So how do you know they're a mink's?"

" 'Cause they were small diamonds in the mud, with five claws," Ashley said.

I was sure I had her. "Yeah, well that could be a weasel or an otter just as easily. Both of them have five toes, too. They look almost exactly the same."

"I looked it up," Ashley said defensively.

"Well, I have to see it myself before I'll believe it," I said, turning back to my breakfast.

"You'll see," Ashley said through yet another mouthful. "I'll prove it to you."

△

CHAPTER 2

△Ashley followed the tracks ever so carefully. I had to give it to her. They certainly *looked* like the tracks from a mink.

The tracks were clear. They were in some mud along the creek that ran through the valley below our houses on the side of a small foothill we all called Ganymede. Jupiter was the nearest town. Ganymede was the name of a satellite moon that circled the planet Jupiter, so we named our little community after that.

"See," Ashley said, kneeling close to the tracks. She was careful not to step in the mud and smudge any of the tracks.

I looked closely. They were small tracks, with five sharp claws as toes. There were four little marks from the heel pad, and some impressions behind from the foot. The four little marks on the heel pad *were* like that of a mink.

"They could be an otter's," I muttered.

"No way," Ashley said vehemently. "An otter has that little web junk around the toes. These claws are clean in the mud. Plus, an otter's track is, like, twice as big."

I looked again. Ashley was right. There was no webbing between the toes, which would mark it as an otter. And it was too small as well.

It wasn't that Ashley was a better tracker than me. It was just that when she was set on something, she learned everything she could about it. And she'd clearly learned everything she could about a mink so she could prove this to me.

"A weasel, maybe?" I offered. "They both make diamonds like this."

"Uh-uh. A weasel has three points on the heel pad. This definitely has four."

I frowned. Ashley had done her homework. This *could* be a mink. I got to my feet. "Let's follow them."

"I have already."

"So where do they go?"

Ashley didn't answer. She started to walk along the creek, again careful not to step across the dainty tracks.

The very neat prints were right along the water's edge. We walked about a foot outside of them. They led to a fallen log with a three-inch hole beneath it.

"Here it is," Ashley said proudly. "Has to be a mink den."

"Could be. They'll use something like this for a temporary den."

When a mink is traveling or hunting, it won't use a den. But even when it's staying in one place, it may only use a den for a day and then move on. Trappers in the Old West had to move around a lot to get them.

It isn't particular about where it will live, either. A hollow tree, a burrow in a stream bank, a log, an abandoned beaver home, even a hole in the ground—it doesn't seem to care. Sometimes one will take over a muskrat den and kill all the previous occupants.

Minks will eat almost anything small—rabbits, moles, bats, chickens, worms, fish. They're quite fierce—they can attack and kill animals larger than themselves.

"Maybe this is where they had babies?" Ashley suggested.

I checked inside. There was indeed a whole bunch of grass inside. It could have been used for that once. But I doubted it at this time of year. We were way past the point in spring where the babies would have been born.

"Maybe once," I grunted. "But not now."

"Let's follow the tracks on the other side."

"There are more?"

"Sure. On both sides."

We walked around to the other side. There were a lot more on the other side, leading down to the water's edge and beyond. We followed them.

That was when the odor hit us. It was clear and unmistakable. It was coming from farther down the creek. I had an idea what it might be.

9

When a mink is fighting, or when it's caught in a trap, it gives off this incredibly musky odor. I'd never smelled it before, but Mark said you can't miss it.

"Do you smell it?" I asked Ashley, looking off down the creek.

"Yeah. Do you think?"

I nodded. "Let's go see."

We both began to hurry down the creek, kicking through the overgrown weeds and undergrowth that clung tenaciously to the banks of the creek. We didn't have to go far.

The trap was just at the water's edge, carefully concealed in the weeds. The trap had clearly been placed along the mink run—or the weasel run. I still wasn't sure what animal it was.

When hunters wanted to catch animals, I knew, they carefully concealed the traps along the paths the animals usually took, along water or a deer track through the woods. Usually they were spring-loaded traps that popped and killed the animal when it tripped over the trap.

The one ranchers and farmers used in the fields and pastures was a walk-on trap, used to kill rats, weasels, and squirrels. It was a square, metal trap with a cocked spring and a metal rod that crushed the animal when it stepped on a footpad in the center of the trap.

But the trap here by the creek wasn't one of those. Ashley and I knelt to take a closer look. I couldn't believe what I was seeing. There were two small wooden sticks pounded in the ground. A thin wire with a small metal ball at one end was tied onto the first stick and looped through a second stick a few inches away.

It was a snare. No one uses snares. They're ancient traps. There are much more modern traps, Mark told me, that kill animals instantly, without a struggle.

Plus, to catch an animal with a snare, you have to place it *exactly* in the right spot, where the small animal runs by. You really have to know what you're doing. You have to know what an animal will do, how it moves, to catch one with a snare.

There was a sudden burst of movement in the grass on the other side of the snare.

Ashley screamed. I practically fell over backward. I stifled my own scream. The hair bristled on the back of my neck. Ashley reached over and gripped my arm.

There was a second burst of movement in the grass, less violent than the first one. We were more prepared this time, and neither of us panicked.

"What is it, do you think?" Ashley whispered.

"Something small," I whispered back. I wasn't sure why we were whispering. It wasn't like the animal was going to run away at the sound of our voices.

I looked more closely at the end of the snare. Sure enough, the animal—whatever it was—had tripped the snare. The looped end of the wire was nowhere to be seen. So it had to be around the end of the animal's foot.

The animal had probably come on the trap during the night, had gotten its foot caught in the loop wire at the end of the snare, and then spent the entire night struggling to free itself. All in vain.

It was probably now completely exhausted from

11

its struggle. It would remain here until another animal, like a fox or a bobcat, came along and killed it, or until the hunter who'd laid the trap came along and killed it.

I felt sorry for the animal. What a rotten way to die. To lie here and struggle for hours and hours, with no hope and no clue what had happened to you. Better to get crushed instantly in a walk-on trap, I figured.

"Let's free it!" Ashley said finally.

I looked over at her. "Are you out of your mind? If it's a mink or a weasel, we'll never get near it. It'll take a big huge bite out of our hand."

Ashley looked back at the trap. "But we can't just leave it here to die. We have to do *something*."

I thought for a moment. If it was a mink, and we tried to take the loop off its ensnared foot, we would almost certainly get bitten. We had no chance of freeing it. But if it was a rabbit, then we had a shot.

I stood up. I looked around for a stick long enough to poke around safely. I found one a few feet away, hopped up and grabbed it, and then came back. "Watch out," I ordered. Ashley took a couple of steps backward and watched me.

I reached over and prodded the grass near the spot where we'd seen the movement. I poked around until the stick hit something soft. There was an instant, violent reaction. The animal spit and squealed at us, then reached up with its head to take a big bite out of the end of the stick. I dropped it.

It was a blue mink. Ashley had been right. The animal had a pointy head and a long neck down to its

12

short front paws. I didn't need to see the rest of its body concealed in the grass. It was definitely a mink.

"What do we do now?" Ashley asked.

I shook my head. There wasn't anything we could do. We weren't going to get close to this animal. We had no chance of freeing it from the snare loop. I picked up the stick again and poked a little more. I got the same reaction from the mink. It was still fighting mad that it had been caught.

"We'll have to leave it," I declared.

"No!" Ashley cried. "We can't do that. We have to free it."

"But there's no way. We'll get bitten."

Ashley looked down at the two sticks driven into the ground. "Then let's pull those up," she suggested.

I looked down at the sticks. We *could* do that. If we pulled the stakes free, the mink could run off and, with any luck, eventually free itself from the loop. It certainly gave the animal a fighting chance.

"But it might turn on us once we've pulled the sticks out," I cautioned.

"We have to try. We just have to. We'll pull them up and then run like crazy."

Ashley had that wild look in her eyes, the one she always got just before she did something crazy, like take a big jump on her bike or climb up some embankment that was probably too steep. There was no stopping her.

I looked back at the sticks. They were rough-hewn, but someone had taken some time to whittle away at them with a knife so they could be driven into the ground more easily. Whoever had laid this trap had

13

taken a little care with it. They wouldn't be pleased if they found we'd let the animal run away with it.

But of course, I reasoned, they wouldn't know we'd done it. Then I looked down at all the footprints we'd left in the area. I laughed out loud.

"What's so funny?" Ashley demanded.

"Oh, I was just thinkin' that maybe the hunter wouldn't know we'd set the animal free, and then I remembered we'd left our own tracks everywhere for the whole world to see."

"Oh." Ashley clearly didn't have a clue what I was talking about. "So are you gonna do it or not?"

I took a deep breath. Might as well, I figured. Ashley clearly wasn't leaving here until we'd freed the dumb thing.

"OK," I muttered. "But you stand back. No need for *both* of us to get bitten."

Ashley nodded and began to walk backward. Her eyes never left me or the snare. I took the stick again and whacked the two stakes. They were solidly in the ground. I'd just have to risk pulling them up. It would place me close enough to the mink that it could come at me if it wanted. But I didn't know any other way to do it.

I dropped the stick and moved in, keeping both eyes riveted on the spot where the mink lay trapped in the grass. Any sudden movement and I was bolting.

I crept up right beside the two sticks. The mink hadn't budged. Slowly, every nerve screaming, I reached down with both hands. I grabbed the two sticks firmly. I sent a quick prayer to God hurtling to the sky and then yanked on the sticks for all I was worth.

The sticks came flying out of the ground. I caught part of the wire of the snare with my hand and dragged the mink about a foot through the grass. It spit, hissed, and squealed like crazy, practically leaping a foot into the air and then landing with a soft *thud* in the grass again.

I yelled once and then sprinted in Ashley's direction. I was absolutely terrified. My throat was dry and constricted. I wanted to just collapse.

"Did you get the trap free?" Ashley asked. Her eyes still hadn't left the spot where the mink was.

"I . . . I think so," I said, completely winded. "I pulled as hard as I could."

We both remained, me gasping for air, Ashley staring intently at the spot where the mink lay.

Finally, after a few minutes, the mink began to stir. It had discovered that it had more movement. I had pulled both sticks free. The snare loop was still around one of the mink's legs, but now that it had discovered it was free, it could walk away.

There was more movement in the grass, then a *splash* in the water of the creek. Ashley hurried toward the creek. I followed.

We both caught sight of the mink as it ran downstream in the creek, the two sticks and snare trailing behind. It had escaped. Now it was only a question of whether it could free its leg from the wire loop before another larger animal could capture it. I figured it had the day to get the job done.

"We did what we could," I said as we watched the mink disappear from sight.

"Yeah, that was cool," Ashley said. "I'm glad we did it."

"Who do you think set the trap?"

Ashley shrugged. "I was thinkin' about that. But I can't figure it."

"I know," I said. "The trap was really well made. But, man, nobody uses traps like that anymore."

Ashley looked back at me. "You ask your dad. I'll ask mine. OK?"

I nodded. "Sure, and we should go talk to Miss Lily also. She'd know, I bet."

There was definitely a mystery here. What I didn't know yet was which way it would turn.

△
CHAPTER 3

△Mark didn't have a clue. Ashley's father hadn't heard of a hunter laying snare traps in this part of the High Sierras for a long time, either.

Oh, there were plenty of folks who laid traps. But they weren't hunters looking for mink pelts, like they used to in the Old West. It was the ranchers and farmers who were sick to death of having their land overrun with rabbits or weasels or whatever who laid those traps.

They lined their fields with either spring-loaded mole traps or walk-on traps that got larger animals as well. There were plenty of those around. I'd seen a few of them rusted out in fields since I'd come out west.

And once, a very long time ago, when America was a younger country, there were hunters everywhere out west, laying traps and catching animals like the one we'd seen.

They caught them and sold their coats for a few dollars each. It was how they managed to pay for the privilege and honor of living out in the wild. They were trappers, mostly, not really hunters.

But those days were long gone. Now minks were raised on mink farms. The minks ate as well as I did, maybe better. Nobody really trapped minks much anymore with snare traps.

So it made no sense. Who had laid the trap? Why? And were there more?

"Beats me," Mark had said. "But I'll ask around. See if anyone's heard anything."

"So you've never heard of someone working traps like that?" I'd pressed at dinner that night.

"Nope. Nobody except the ranchers laying them in their fields. Oh, I guess there are a few old-timers who might put traps out. But it's mostly for recreation."

"Recreation?"

"Sure. For fun, I guess. They learned how to trap when they were kids, so now they do it for fun."

"Really?"

"Well, actually, I'm just guessing," Mark had mused. "I've never really heard of anyone doing that kind of thing."

I hadn't bought that argument, and I wasn't sure Mark did either. "Who would do that for fun?"

Mark had shrugged. "Probably you're right. I guess it wouldn't make too much sense to do all of that just for fun."

"Yeah, I mean who kills animals for fun, anyway?"

Mark had thought for a long time. "It sounds like somebody, maybe some kids, who're just foolin' around. I don't know."

Mark and I were planning a four-day camping trip in a few days, when he had a couple of days off coming to him. We'd been planning it for weeks.

Since Mark had married my mom, he and I really hadn't spent a whole huge amount of time together. We talked, I guess. But it wasn't like we were best friends or anything. And he wasn't my dad. He was my stepdad.

My dad had died three years ago. I still found myself remembering things that had happened, that only we had shared.

I saw a lot of Mark during the day because I was working at the ranger station some. Mostly I hung out at the main cabin and listened to the rangers talk, ran errands, junk like that. I'd been doing that for a couple of weeks. It was pretty cool.

Mark and I still hadn't decided where to go camping for our four-day trip. We'd narrowed it down to two possible trails, both of them just a few miles from a road that ended at the Hopewell ranger station, but well into the wilderness.

One trail went north from the ranger station, through the Timberline Gap. It went over the divide separating the middle and east forks of the Hialeah River and descended into Rocky Mount Creek Canyon. From there, you could take the White Rock Pass trail to the High Sierra trail at Little Arroyo junction.

Mark said we'd have no problem hiking on that route. It was about seventeen miles to the junction, and there was almost no chance of snow through White Rock Pass.

But the trail I wanted to take went straight east from the Hopewell ranger station. It was called the Sabertooth trail, and it ran through King Lakes up to Sabertooth Peak at more than twelve thousand feet. From there, the trail wound down to the huge Columbia Lake.

The problem, Mark said, is that Sabertooth Pass is usually filled with snow in early summer. Sometimes you can't get to the lake until late July. Mark was checking to see if we could make it.

I hoped so. I figured it would be cool to go through a pass and up to a mountain that was twelve thousand feet high. I'd never hiked anything like it, ever. Plus, from the lake we'd get a chance to go into Ghost Canyon and, eventually, to the High Sierra trail.

It was about twenty miles for that trip. Mark figured if we made ten miles a day, we could go out and back in four days. He thought I was old enough to make such a trip. I wasn't so sure.

Ashley decided we had to ask Miss Lily about the traps. She'd know, Ashley said. She'd know for sure.

Miss Lily was an old, old Indian woman who lived by herself in a log cabin in a big pasture on land that had once been owned by her ancestors. The government owned the land now, but they looked the other way and let her live on it.

Miss Lily seemed to know everything about animals. She knew how they thought, how they'd react in almost any situation. It had probably been forever since she'd tracked an animal the way Ashley and I did. But she still knew.

We both knew the way to her cabin by heart now. It wasn't too far from Ganymede, actually. It only took us about ten minutes on our bikes, along a couple of shortcuts through the woods.

Miss Lily was out in her garden when we arrived. She was bent over, digging with something. She didn't look up as we arrived.

"Joshua Landis," she said softly, "I need that small pouch."

I ditched my bike and hurried over to her side. I looked around. There was a small pouch a few feet from her. I scooped it up and handed it to her.

"How'd you know it was me?" I asked.

Miss Lily smiled, but still didn't look up. "And how would I *not* know it was you? The whole world hears you approach."

I scowled. "It's just my bike. The chain rattles. I'm real quiet when I'm walking in the forest."

Miss Lily glanced over. "You are?"

"Yeah, pretty quiet."

"So you could catch a deer with your bare hands?"

"Nobody could do that," I protested.

"Nobody?"

"Nobody I know."

"And you're sure of this?"

I stared at her. "No way *you* could do that."

Miss Lily looked down at her little garden. "Not now. But once, many moons ago. When I was much younger."

"You could sneak up on a deer?" I asked, more than a little incredulous.

21

"I could."

Ashley parked her bike and joined us. "I believe her. If Miss Lily says she could do it, then it's gotta be true."

"What's in the pouch?" I asked, deciding to change the subject.

"Life," Miss Lily said.

"Felt like seeds to me," I said.

"And that is not life?"

"Not right away, it isn't."

"And what is 'right away' to you, Joshua Landis?"

"Um, I don't know. A while. It takes forever for those things to sprout."

"Forever?"

"Yeah. You can't see those dumb things actually do anything." I was feeling ornery for some reason. I couldn't explain it. Maybe it was because I always felt like Miss Lily gave me a hard time just for fun.

Miss Lily rummaged through her pouch and pulled a slightly orange seed from it. She pressed the top with her thumbnail and then handed it to me. "There's a cup of water on the porch. Go put this in it."

"Why?"

"Go," Miss Lily commanded.

I took the small seed, turned on my heel, and jogged over to the small porch at the front of her little cabin. I found the cup of water and dropped the seed into it. Then I hurried back to the garden.

Ashley and Miss Lily had begun to talk about traps. Ashley was describing the snare trap we'd come across.

22

"What did the two sticks look like?" Miss Lily asked.

"They were whittled down," Ashley said.

"With a knife?"

"Yeah, I think," answered Ashley. "That's what it looked like."

"And the rope? What was it made of?"

Ashley looked over at me. "Wire, right?"

I nodded. "It felt like a thin wire when I yanked it up from the ground."

"You're sure it was a wire?"

I thought back to the incident. The wire—if that was what it was—had been extremely thin. It suddenly occurred to me what it looked like. "I know what it was," I said, excited.

"What?" Miss Lily asked.

"It was a guitar string. I'm sure of it."

"And why is that?" Miss Lily asked.

What I had remembered was the little metal ball at the end of the wire. It had seemed odd at the time. Now it made perfect sense. I described the little ball at the end of the wire.

"You're right," Ashley exclaimed. "It had to be a guitar string."

"But who would rip up their guitar to do that?" I asked.

"And why would they set a trap like that in the first place?" Ashley asked.

Miss Lily didn't say anything right away. She finished her task. She was laying seeds carefully in a row she'd dug. She was placing the seeds in a small trench. She dropped one seed in carefully about every six inches.

Finally, she straightened up. She looked over at me. "Would you mind covering the seeds?"

"With dirt?"

"What would you cover them with?"

"Dirt, I guess," I muttered. I knelt down and started to scoop up handfuls of dirt and toss them into the trench. Ashley knelt down and helped too. It didn't take us long to fill in what Miss Lily had just dug.

"Now some water," she said.

I took the water jug and started at one end. "How much?"

"Make the ground wet," she said. "So you can see the water sitting on the ground."

I did as she said, pouring enough so that I could see little pools of water forming over the trench she'd dug. I walked along the trench, pouring as I went.

This definitely wasn't my thing. Ashley seemed to like it, though. She sometimes came out here just to help Miss Lily with her garden.

Miss Lily got nearly all of her food from this garden. Ashley and I sometimes brought her stuff, just in case. Like flour so she could make bread. Or potatoes and apples.

Miss Lily started to walk toward the edge of the forest, in the direction of a stand of pines. Ashley and I followed.

She stopped at the edge and looked off into the forest. We stood near her side. "So this trap, was it laid well?" she asked.

Ashley and I looked at each other. "Um, yeah, I guess so," I said finally.

"Was it where the animal would run?"

"Yeah, it was right near the mink's den," Ashley said.

"A fresh den?" Miss Lily asked.

"I don't know," I said. "How can you tell if the den's fresh?"

Miss Lily didn't look over. "Did you check for signs that the mink had been there recently?"

"There were tracks," I said defensively.

"How old?"

"I dunno," I mumbled. "They seemed fresh."

"You're sure?"

"No, I'm not sure. But the mud wasn't dry yet. And the tracks were right there."

Miss Lily smiled. "That's a start. They were probably fresh, then. But the den. How was it?"

"There was grass inside," Ashley offered.

"Dry grass, or with twigs, too?"

"Dry grass, I think," Ashley said. "I don't think there were twigs."

"Any other signs?"

"Nope," I said. "But we didn't check all that much."

Miss Lily looked over at me for a moment. It was enough. I could see it in her eyes. She was disappointed in me. I *should* have looked. I should have spent more time trying to understand what nature was telling me.

"Next time, perhaps?" she asked me softly.

"Next time," I promised, holding her gaze.

Miss Lily looked back at the forest. "And this trap, was it on the run, or just off it, hidden in the weeds?"

"Just next to it, in the weeds," Ashley said.

"Hidden well?"

"Yeah, we had to look a little to spot it," I said.

"Close to the den?"

"A few feet away," I answered. "It was pretty close."

Miss Lily nodded. "It is a real trapper, then."

"A real trapper?" I asked.

"Someone who knows the ways of animals."

"How do you know?"

Miss Lily looked back at us. "It is hard to get near a mink den unobserved. You must know when the mink is there, and when it isn't. And to conceal a trap, yet still catch your animal, that is a trick you learn with much wisdom."

I nodded. "And whoever laid this trap got it close to the den, plus kept it hidden."

"Yes," Miss Lily said.

"So the hunter must know animals pretty well," Ashley chipped in.

"Yes, like the trappers my ancestors knew," Miss Lily said quietly.

"What do you think it means?" I asked.

"I don't know," she answered. "But time will give you its answer. Now it is time to show you a mystery." She started to walk back toward her porch.

"What mystery?" I asked.

"Life," Miss Lily said.

When we got to the porch, Miss Lily sat down in her chair. "Go look at the cup of water, where you placed the seed."

Ashley and I hurried over. I looked inside. The seed had changed. It was no longer just a seed. A little green shoot had begun to emerge from the spot where Miss Lily had pressed her thumbnail.

"Cool," Ashley said.

I just stared at the tiny little seed. As usual, Miss Lily had taught me something I had not asked for.

"Quickly, Joshua," Miss Lily ordered. "Go plant it with the others."

I ran over to the trench, dug a little hole, and placed the seed with the green shoot in the ground. I smiled to myself. So it didn't take so long after all to witness life. Not long at all.

When I returned, Miss Lily nodded solemnly. "Life," she said.

I nodded back. "Life. I understand now."

Miss Lily folded her hands. "The trapper you are searching for will be like that. You must watch carefully. Watch for the signs. Only then will the identity be revealed."

"Just watch?"

"Yes, watch. Look for the signs. They are there. They are always there," Miss Lily said.

CHAPTER 4

△OK, so I'd watch for the signs. I had absolutely no idea what to watch for. But what else was new? It seemed like I was always stumbling around in the dark, trying to figure out what was going on. Everyone seemed to know. Except me.

I went with Mark to Ranger Station #3 the next morning. I rode with him in his four-wheel-drive Jeep Cherokee.

I liked the way the Jeep took the hard ruts on the dirt road. The wheels just sort of caromed off the ruts —*bang, bang, bang, bang*—and then kept rolling. If one wheel spun out, the others picked up the slack.

I could see that Mark liked driving the four-wheel, too. Sometimes, just for fun, he'd veer off the road and wander through the brush and the weeds beside the road. I hung on. He grinned like the Cheshire cat.

Mark was still learning how to be a National Park Service ranger. He had some training in Washington, D.C., before we moved out west to California. It was his second career. He'd been a construction worker for years until he'd met my mom.

I could see he loved his job. It was Mark. He liked being outside, not cooped up inside over a desk. He loved roaming the woods, either by foot or by Jeep. It made no difference to him, as long as he was outside.

I'd never really thought about it much, whether you were inside or out. But I guess it made a difference. Mom said there were some people who just had to work outside. It wasn't that they were claustrophobic. They just had to be outside.

Mark was one of those people. He brooded when he was inside. He radiated when he stepped out the door. He came alive, like a flower reaching for the sun.

Mark always took great care to lace up his boots. He took pride in how they were polished. He always made sure his pants were creased, that his belt fit snugly around his waist, that his dark green shirt had no wrinkles, that his tie was straight.

Mark was proud of his life as a ranger. He thought he was doing God's work, caring for nature. He didn't revere it. He didn't believe animals were higher than mankind, or anything crazy like that.

No, he took the Bible's commands about nature and animals literally. Our job was to nurture the animals and the Earth. It was our job to care for it, not destroy it. Mark took those commands very, very seriously.

I knew people had wild ideas about nature. Mom

30

said that was natural. It was easy to get things all mixed up sometimes. People started to worship things they really shouldn't.

It was like that with nature. People saw the beauty and majesty of nature, and they saw only the creation. They did not see the Creator.

It was even easier to fall into that trap out in the Sierra Nevadas, Mom said. In a place where mountains tower as high as fourteen thousand feet into the sky, where huge sequoia trees are twenty-five feet across and nearly three hundred feet tall, where every wild creature in North America roams freely and where rivers run through valleys that look more like cathedrals than anything else, it was easy to fall in love with the creation and ignore the Creator.

Mark and I were going to see some of those giant trees when we went camping and hiking for four days. We would at least drive past an area where the sequoias grew very tall.

Mark said the largest he'd ever heard of had a diameter of thirty-five feet, and had been measured at 325 feet. That just absolutely blew my mind. That was taller than a football field was long. And it was about as wide as our house.

Mark also said these giants could live as long as five thousand years. It took quite a disaster to kill one of those big trees.

That meant that there were sequoias alive today that were also around during Old Testament times, and when Jesus walked the Earth. But those trees told no tales. They were silent witnesses to the ever-changing tides of the Earth and men—always present, always vigilant.

31

Where we lived, there weren't any sequoias—just pines, spruces, and firs. They were still big, though, compared to the tiny things on the East Coast, where I'd lived most of my life. They were probably twice as big here.

As Mark and I drove through the forest toward Ranger Station #3, it occurred to me that my life had changed an awful lot in just a few short months.

I was no longer the same kid I'd been. I was more at ease outdoors, not so intimidated or frightened by the wild, rugged elements of nature. I felt like I could hold my own.

Of course, just when I got to feeling like I could stand on my own two feet, something would come along and scare the bewillikers out of me. Like a grizzly towering over me, or the blood-curdling cry of a cougar protecting its offspring, or a forest fire raging out of control.

Nature was like that. Almost like heaven one moment, teetering on the edge of the abyss the next. They said the ocean could be that way too. Calm, peaceful, serene one minute, and a raging cauldron of trouble in the midst of a storm the next.

Mark lurched to the right, avoiding a boulder. I gripped the side door handle. Mark righted the Jeep an instant later. "Sorry," he said, laughing. "Didn't want to take out the front axle."

"No problem," I answered.

Mark glanced over at me. "You like working at the station?"

"Yeah, sure."

"You don't mind Mr. Wilson?"

Mr. Wilson was Mark's boss. He was an old hand.

He'd been a ranger forever. He knew everything about everything. Once, when a bear had been on the rampage and the rangers had tried to find it before it killed someone, Mr. Wilson and I had gone out together. A Land Rover had flipped over onto him, and I'd found the bear. Mr. Wilson had never quite forgiven me for that little episode. Or at least that's what he said when he teased me about it.

But I liked Mr. Wilson. He always took the time to explain stuff to me, even when he was real busy.

"Nah, he's OK," I answered.

"You're sure?"

"Yeah. Mr. Wilson's OK."

Mark nodded and returned to his driving. "Say. By the way, some of the rangers say there *have* been more traps around lately. They've been turning up a few miles into the wilderness."

That got my attention. "Yeah? Like what?"

A scowl crossed Mark's face. "A couple of the rangers said they've come across a whole lot more of those steel-jaw leghold traps."

"What kinda trap?"

"Steel-jaw leghold," Mark repeated.

"What's that?"

Mark slowed the Jeep a little. "It's a different kind of trap. It's made to preserve the hide of the animal, so when it's skinned it won't have any teeth marks in it."

I looked over at Mark. I really had no idea what he was talking about. "What do you mean, no teeth marks? What's that mean? Why's it important?"

Mark sighed. "OK. Imagine there's a big trap, big enough to crush an animal. The trap springs and the jaws of the trap kill the animal—say it's a mink—but it also cuts right through the skin. That pelt is worthless to a trapper. He needs a pelt that's intact, to make any money off it."

"But I thought there weren't any trappers around."

Mark shook his head. "Oh, there are still trappers. Not as many. But there are still some. And a few of the rangers have been telling me they're starting to come back into the wilderness."

"Come back?"

"Sort of like a revival. Back to nature. There are more of them starting to come back, live in the wilderness. Live off the land, that sort of thing."

"Really?"

"Yeah, really. And they make a little money, enough to keep them going, by trapping and selling some of the hides."

I thought about it for a second. I was beginning to understand. "But the hide has to be perfect, right?"

Mark nodded. "Right. And a leghold trap does the trick."

"How?"

"When the animal's leg is trapped, caught by the steel jaws," Mark explained, "it keeps the animal there until the trapper arrives. The steel jaws are powerful enough to hold the animal there, but it doesn't trap the body."

"And then?"

"Then the trapper arrives, usually kills the animal with a blow to the head—he doesn't want to put a bullet hole in the hide, either—and then he has a hide that's intact."

"Hmmm," I muttered.

"The only problem with those stupid steel-jaw leghold traps is that the animals sometimes freak out when they're caught in one of them."

"Like how?" I'd never heard of this before.

"A really fierce animal will go crazy if it's caught in a leghold trap. It'll run around in a circle, or spin around and around until its leg comes off. Or, sometimes, it'll chew its own leg off."

"Come *on!* You're not serious?"

"I wish," Mark grunted. "But it's true. Those leghold traps can really torture an animal until the trapper shows up to check on it. A couple of the rangers have found leghold traps with paws left behind, just in the last two weeks, I heard."

I took a deep breath. This was hard for me to imagine. I could understand killing animals. That was just the way it was. But this seemed a little different. I couldn't quite sort it out.

"Are those traps, like, illegal?"

Mark shook his head. "Nope. Not in this country they're not. It's perfectly legal. If I had my way—and I think most of the rangers feel this way if you asked 'em—they wouldn't be. But they are, and more and more people are starting to use them again."

I thought about this for the whole rest of the trip to the ranger station. It seemed absolutely crazy to me. Just when the whole world was going crazy with videos and computers and fax machines and just about every electronic gizmo you could possibly dream up, there were more people trying to live off the land in the wilderness.

In a strange way, it *did* make sense. When you were stuck in front of the TV, or at a computer, it

35

was kind of unreal. When you were outdoors, everything was a whole lot more real. I could understand how people wanted to escape.

In the Old West, they were called mountain men. They lived in the wilderness the whole year round and only came out to sell their animal hides or get a few provisions. Then they'd melt back into the wilderness for another year.

So the mountain men had come back? Were there such people again in the Sierra Nevadas? I guessed I'd find out.

CHAPTER 5

△When we got to the ranger station, Mark had to go out almost immediately. There was a report of a half-crazed creature attacking a mule train along one of the main trails. Mr. Wilson wanted someone to check it out, and Mark got picked.

I begged to go along. In the end, Mr. Wilson caved in and agreed to let me go. It wasn't like the situation was dangerous, he reasoned. I didn't argue.

Lee Samuels and another ranger I didn't know real well, Ryan, came along. It took us close to an hour to find the mule train. We had to cut back on three different trails until we were able to pick up the main one where the report had come from.

The mule train was camped off to the side of the road when we arrived. The small party was milling

37

around. Two of the people came running up to us as our Land Rover arrived.

"Hurry! Please hurry!" a young man with a beard and a ponytail yelled at us. "It was a badger, with rabies! Our friend was bitten!"

We all piled out of the Rover. Lee sprinted over to a knot of people who were crowded around a young man. By the time I arrived, he was at the man's side, examining the wound.

"What was it?" Mark asked the people. There were about a dozen or so, I counted.

"A badger. Definitely," one of them offered.

I glanced over at the mules, grazing just off to the side of the trail. I knew the rangers hated mule trains. They trampled the trails. But they were legal, and people still used pack trains to get through the wilderness.

The mules were still clearly agitated by the attack. One of them let loose with an ornery, plaintive *Bray!* while I was looking. They didn't much like what was happening.

"Yeah, it was definitely a badger," someone else said. "And it was crazy. It just came running at us."

"It just went right after his leg," a third person said, gesturing toward the man, who was sitting on the ground, a ripped shirt around his leg as a tourniquet.

"Where's the badger now?" Ryan asked.

"Ran off," answered the first person we'd come across.

"Anything unusual about it?" Lee asked.

"Yeah, man, it had blood everywhere, all over it," said the man with the ponytail. "And it was stumbling all over itself as it ran toward us, like there was something wrong with it."

Mark and I looked at each other at the same moment. We were both thinking exactly the same thing.

"Can you show me where the badger ran at you?" I asked him.

"Yeah, sure, man. Follow me."

Mark and I followed, while Lee attended to the man who'd been bitten and Ryan continued to question the other people.

I could see the tracks clearly even before we'd gotten to the spot where the attack had occurred. The badger had come at the party from the woods, bitten the man, and then run back into the trees.

I knelt down and examined the tracks, ignoring the others for the moment. I looked at them quite carefully. There was no mistaking what had happened here. It was as plain as the nose on my face.

There were three very clear tracks in the dirt, where three healthy legs had touched the ground. Then there was a fourth print, from a badly injured leg.

The badger had been caught in one of those traps—a steel-jaw leghold trap. It was eerie. Mark and I had just been talking about it, and then this. It was really, really strange.

The track from the injured leg was different from the other three. There was no clear print, just a smudge from where the injured paw had scraped or brushed the ground. I followed the tracks. The others were just like the one I'd first examined.

I walked over to Mark. He'd seen the same thing. He nodded at me silently. I didn't say anything. We

39

waited until the man with the ponytail had rejoined his friends and Mark and I were alone.

"It's just like you were telling me, isn't it?" I asked him.

Mark nodded. "It's incredible. We were just talking about it, and then we run across this."

"The badger was caught in one of those, um, those . . . ?"

"Steel-jaw leghold traps? Yeah, it looks that way. Somehow it got free, and then viciously attacked this mule train out of blind rage."

"Man, I don't blame it," I said quietly.

"Me neither. But we have to find that badger and destroy it."

"I can help," I said eagerly. "I can track it."

Mark looked over at me. "You think?"

"I *know* I can."

"Well, then"—Mark smiled—"have at it. Lee can stay behind, with all these folks. You can come with Ryan and me to track this badger."

Badgers, I knew, lived mostly in the West. They were fierce, powerful fighters. They didn't have many enemies. Just the bears and cougars, mostly. One badger can hold its own against a pack of dogs.

A badger has a heavy body, for its size—they're only about two feet long—with a short, bushy tail, a white stripe and patches on its face, and long claws on the front of its paws.

Badgers like to burrow and tunnel after small rodents. They'll eat snakes, birds, even birds' eggs. They have their babies in the spring, and they're all grown up by the fall.

There really isn't any other creature like a badger.

It digs like crazy, thanks to its long claws. It can burrow way underground, with long tunnels. If this badger went back to its burrow, we'd never get to it. But I doubted it was burrowed just now.

It was too bad it had been a badger that had come along and been captured by that leghold trap. A badger's fur was just about worthless as a hide. But I guess that's what a trapper bargains for. Sometimes a trap caught animals that weren't worth anything to people as fur coats.

I knew it was unusual to find a badger up here in the mountains. Usually, the badgers liked to stay down in the grassy valleys, even out in the deserts on the other side of the mountains. But sometimes, if food was scarce, they'd drift into the mountains. It was too bad this badger had made that choice.

I wasn't real sure what we'd do once we found this badger. It was likely to be half-crazed still. It would likely attack us once we'd found it. I looked over at Mark to make sure he was carrying his gun. He was. I breathed a sigh of relief.

I'd used a gun once in my life, to kill a bear that had attacked a five-year-old boy. I'd borrowed the gun from a ranger only because I didn't have any choice. When I'd fired the gun, it had nearly knocked me over. But I had killed the bear. I would never forget what had happened that day.

Ryan joined us a couple of minutes later. He'd finished questioning the party. They'd all pretty much seen the same thing. There was no mistaking it. A half-crazed badger had come charging at the man and taken a big bite out of his leg.

"Well, let's roll," Mark said. He looked over at me. "Ready to give it a shot?"

I nodded. I was really nervous. I'd never actually tracked something like this, in this kind of a situation. Usually, I just tried to follow a dog's track, or maybe a cat's. I'd come across the tracks of a fox, or a skunk, or a raccoon, an occasional possum. But never a badger.

It wasn't going to be hard to follow, though. The badger's front claws were so long they took a huge line in the mud, especially now when it was running. I began to track the badger. Mark and Ryan followed behind silently.

I knew they were both able to follow the badger better than I could. At least that's what I figured. Mark knew plenty about tracking. He talked to me about it a lot.

But they were letting me go after this myself. They both had their guns out, with the safeties on, just in case. They wouldn't stun the badger when we found it—or if we found it. They'd kill it outright and put it out of its misery.

The badger wasn't following any particular line. It was running scared and angry, from tree to bush and back out into the open again. Its line zigzagged all over the place.

After a while, though, I could see that something else was happening to the badger. Its step started to get shorter. It must have started walking. Then its bloody print started to show up more in the track, which told me that the badger was really beginning to tire, forced to rely more on its injured leg as it walked.

After a mile or so, I could see that the badger was exhausted and probably at the end of its rope. The tracks were quite short, just a few inches apart, and deep in the ground. It was walking heavy.

When the tracks disappeared into a very thick growth of underbrush and shrubs on the side of a hill, I turned and looked at Mark. We all knew. The badger had to be in there. This was, most likely, its final resting place.

"Should we get it to come out?" Ryan asked Mark.

Mark nodded his head. "I guess we'll have to. We can't just assume it'll die in there."

"So what do we do?" I asked.

Mark smiled at me. "By the way, that was a great job. You did a wonderful job of leading us here."

I beamed. But I didn't take too much time to dwell on his compliment. There was still a lot of work to be done, and I had no idea what either Mark or Ryan would do.

Ryan looked over at the thick stand of shrubs, nestled among some big pines. "It has to be in there. I'll bet it didn't even try to dig a burrow."

"I think you're right," Mark agreed. "It probably collapsed."

"We can't just go in," Ryan said. "That would be too dangerous."

I suddenly had an idea. I looked around. There were heavy pine cones on the ground. It wasn't the time of year when cones were supposed to fall, but there were always a few lying around. I began to stuff them in my pocket.

"What're you doin'?" Mark asked.

43

"I have an idea," I said, still stuffing pine cones into my pockets.

"Now don't do anything crazy just yet," Mark warned.

"No, don't worry," I reassured him. "This is totally safe. You'll see."

When I'd finished gathering pine cones, I explained my idea to Mark and Ryan quickly. When I was finished, they both nodded in agreement. It was worth a shot.

I was going to climb one of the pine trees near the edge of the shrubs and undergrowth. I could shinny up the tree and then look down into the undergrowth. Once I had an eagle's eye view of the place, I was going to start dropping pine cones until I saw some movement. Then I would let Mark and Ryan know where the badger was. I had no idea whether it would work. But it was worth a try, I figured.

I started up the nearest tree. It was hard work, especially with two pockets stuffed to bursting with pine cones, but eventually I got up to the first level of branches with nothing more than a couple of scraped hands and a bruised knee to show for my efforts.

I climbed out onto the first heavy branch that would support my weight and surveyed the landscape below me. From up here, it looked different, not as thick with shrubs.

I couldn't see the badger. But there were some obvious hiding places—patches where the shrubs grew thick around another tree, for instance.

I started to heave pine cones down at the spot. I emptied one entire pocket with no results, other than one bird I frightened away from a nearby tree and a chattering squirrel.

Then, about three pine cones into my second pocket, I hit pay dirt. The cone landed squarely in the middle of a big shrub about twenty feet into the undergrowth and there was a furious, vicious rustle in response. It had to be the badger.

"Got it!" I yelled down.

"Where?" Mark called up.

I pointed my finger at the spot, then at the nearest tree. "See that tree?" Mark followed my finger, and then nodded. "Well, it's right under it."

Mark and Ryan talked for a moment. Then Mark looked up at me. "Josh, I want you to stay up there. You'll be safe there. Keep an eye out for anything strange. Holler if you see it."

I nodded and then watched what they were going to do. I knew they had to flush the badger out somehow. I figured there was probably only one way to do this—by spooking it—and it looked like that's exactly what Mark and Ryan were going to do.

They both released the safeties on their guns. Ryan started to work his way around to the other side of the tree. They'd come at it from opposite directions, and then start doing whatever they could to distract the badger and get it to emerge from the shrubs.

When they were in position, Mark called up to me again. "Josh, start tossing more pine cones in there, see what happens."

I pulled more cones from my pocket and started firing away. A couple didn't hit the target, but once I got the range, I started to hit the spot with deadly accuracy.

45

There was a lot of rustling and movement, but the badger refused to emerge. Finally, Mark picked up a heavy boulder and heaved it at the undergrowth.

There was a big *thud*, followed immediately by a loud, guttural growl. The badger charged from the spot an instant later, directly at Mark.

"Mark, look out!" I yelled.

But Mark didn't need my warning. He'd seen the badger plainly. He already had his gun raised and pointed at the ground. He fired three times at the badger as it charged toward him. Two of the shots hit their target and stopped the badger dead in its tracks.

The badger spun once in the air and then collapsed. Mark was an expert shot, and he wasn't about to miss at this close range.

I climbed down the tree as fast as I could and hurried over. Ryan arrived at the spot a moment later.

We all knelt to look at the dead badger. It was gross. The badger had obviously gone crazy trying to get free of the trap. I was glad we'd found it and put the poor, pitiful creature out of its misery.

"I want to find that trap," Mark said, standing up. "I want to see it for myself." He looked over at me. "Think you can find it?"

"Sure," I said. "I know I can."

"Great. Then let's roll," Mark said, grim-faced. He wasn't pleased about any of this. But he'd done the job he had to do.

I looked down at the badger one last time. I just shook my head. It seemed like such a waste.

CHAPTER 6

△Following the badger's tracks back to the steel-jaw leghold trap proved harder than I'd thought. The problem was that we had to return to the camp where the badger had attacked the man's leg, and then try to pick up the trail from there. But there were so many tracks in that camp it was hard to pinpoint where the badger trail came in from.

Finally, though, Mark picked it up about twenty feet outside of the perimeter. It had been moving pretty fast when it came into camp, and its marks were all over the ground, not in any orderly fashion.

It was strange backtracking an animal that I now knew was dead. I couldn't explain it, really. It just seemed strange to me somehow.

When the badger had come into the camp, it had obviously been in a rage. It had been running practically at full stride, because its claw marks were quite deep and its gait was long.

I'd figured the stride would get shorter as we moved away from the camp. But it didn't. The badger, it seemed, had worked its way free of the trap and then rushed from the spot straight into the camp, where it had attacked the first person it had come across.

I could tell when we started to get close to the trap, because every fourth track was blood-soaked. As we got closer, there was more caked blood on the ground.

Finally, we came into a small clearing in the middle of the woods, a patch of wild grass and weeds where the badger had probably had its burrow.

We were all shocked at what we saw. There, directly in the middle of the clearing, was a huge hole. It was as if a bulldozer had been dropped right in the middle of the woods and had dug out a huge, perfectly circular hole.

The hole was probably three feet deep or so. It was probably ten feet across. We edged closer. I knew this was the place. It reeked of sheer terror and pain. The badger had clearly been here.

Directly in the middle of the huge hole was the steel-jaw leghold trap. I could see it from the rim of the hole. I stepped down into the hole and moved toward the center to get a better look.

The trap had been staked to the ground. Even with the badger's clearly ferocious efforts, the trap had held.

The trap itself was at the edge of the hole. I moved over and knelt down beside it. Sure enough, tufts of the badger's fur were still left in the steel jaws of the trap.

There were some strange prints around the edge, near the trap. It looked like imprints of tennis shoes —small, maybe about my size. And there were a couple of different kinds. I couldn't tell if it meant anything, though, because they were very faint.

It was obvious what had happened here. The trapper had set the trap near the badger's burrow, most likely. The badger had gotten its leg caught, and then wound itself around and around trying to free its paw, digging a deeper and deeper hole.

"Holy smokes," Ryan said softly as he knelt down beside me. "Never seen anything like *this*."

"Me neither," Mark said.

I looked up at Mark. "Do you know what kind of trap this is?"

Mark examined the trap more closely. He let out a low whistle. "Man, oh, man," he muttered.

"What?" I asked sharply.

"Look at this," Mark said. He pried the trap open, and then lifted the trap up so I could see it. "This is an old, old trap."

We all looked at it. Sure enough, the entire trap was covered with red rust that flaked off as we touched it. It was ancient. But the metal was obviously still tough enough to hold a badger in place for a long time.

It was smaller than I'd have expected. It had a small round metal plate in the middle, where the animal was supposed to step, and a metal rod with two nearly square extensions welded onto it that trapped the animal's leg and held it in place. There was also a powerful spring that exerted pressure downward and kept the trap clamped tight once it had been sprung.

Mark flipped it over and looked at something on the bottom. "Hey, Ryan, ever seen anything like this?"

Ryan looked at it too. He shook his head. "Nope, never heard of them. Not a brand I've ever seen before."

"Can I see it, too?" I asked.

"Sure." Mark held it out so I could see. There was the name of a company etched on the bottom, in raised letters. That was the only way the name was still there, because with so much rust a printed name would have been erased a long time ago.

"Surelock, Inc." was the name of the company that had made the trap. There were elaborate curlicues beneath the letters. "This the name of the company?" I asked.

"Most likely," Ryan answered.

Mark stood up. He began to tug on the trap. He strained with everything he was worth. The trap held. It was almost as if the thing was bolted in place.

Mark dropped the trap and walked toward the center of the huge hole the badger had dug out. He began to work at the dirt around the stake. "Josh, toss me a stick I can use to dig with."

I scrambled out of the hole, searched for a moment, and then tossed a short stick to him.

"Thanks," Mark said. He dug with it for a couple of minutes, until he'd taken up enough dirt so that the stake could be worked free. Then he stood up, pulled on the stake hard, and the thing finally came out. Dirt flew in all directions.

Mark knelt over and picked up the stake. He just shook his head. "Ryan, check this out."

I hurried over too. Mark held a rusted-metal stake in his hand. It was long. The end that had been driven into the ground was flat, like the end of a screwdriver, only a lot larger.

Ryan grunted. "You know what it reminds me of? A railroad spike. My grandpa used to have a few of these around. From after World War I, when they did a whole bunch of railroad stuff, he said."

The end of the chain that held the trap was welded onto the top of the railroad spike—if, in fact, that was what it was. Whoever had done this had wanted to make sure the trap didn't go anywhere.

"Boy, this is strange." Mark shook his head. "I can't ever remember seeing anything like this."

"Me neither," Ryan said.

I looked from the spike, to the trap, and then to Mark. "What does it mean? What is all this?"

"I wish I knew," Mark said softly. "But I don't have a clue."

△

CHAPTER 7

△Ashley was racking her brain. But mostly she was furious at me. How could I *possibly* go on such a great adventure without her? How could I do that?

"But I was at the ranger station with Mark," I protested lamely. "It just happened."

"Well, don't do it again," she said fiercely.

"But, Ashley—"

"I *mean* it," she said, glaring at me with the most intense look she could muster.

I tried not to smile. "All right, but there really was nothin' I could do about it."

"Yeah," she said glumly. "But you didn't have to actually go there, did you?"

I sighed. "Ashley, are you gonna help me figure out about this trap or not?"

Ashley turned her attention back to the *World En-*

53

cyclopedia in front of her. We were in Ashley's house, in her dad's den off to one side of their house. We were searching frantically through the books her dad had there for information on the kind of trap I'd seen earlier that day.

I didn't figure we'd come across anything that would tell us what "Surelock" was. That was too much to hope for. But I figured we'd at least come across things that told us about the kind of trap that had been used.

There wasn't much, though. There was a section about different kinds of traps that had been used over the years. But not much on either steel-jaw leghold traps, or even the snare Ashley and I had come across.

I was really pretty surprised to find that millions of animals were still trapped every year. The kind of steel-jaw traps that had gotten the badger were apparently still used a lot.

They were not, however, really used where we lived. In fact, no one had trapped much throughout the Sierra Nevadas for a long time. The reason, Mark said, was that rangers looked out for the endangered animals living in the Sierras. Trappers didn't want to risk run-ins with the rangers, so they took their traps elsewhere.

But some trapper was here now. That was obvious.

Steel-jaw traps were against the law in a whole bunch of other countries, but not in ours. I couldn't find out why. They just weren't, it seemed.

I guess I mostly figured that they shouldn't be using those kinds of traps. The more I got to know

54

about animals in the wilderness, the more I guess I believed that you had to treat them with respect.

If you were going to kill an animal, well, then you should just kill it—quickly, humanely, without a huge amount of pain and terror for the animal. That steel-jaw leghold contraption had clearly made the badger's last hours a nightmare.

I understood why trappers used them. The encyclopedia said the same thing that Mark had: these traps were used because they kept the hide intact, which is what helped the trapper make money. But the books also said there are other ways to trap animals.

Mostly, there were all sorts of snares, more modern than the one Ashley and I had come across that had trapped the mink. They were attached to different kinds of springs that caught and held an animal without causing it to freak out until the trapper arrived.

Basically, the big difference seemed to be between the kind of traps with steel jaws that really mashed down on animals' legs, and snares that held the animals in place without a whole lot of pain until the trapper got there.

The Indians used something totally different two hundred years ago. They used deadfalls. The way you set up a deadfall was pretty simple, actually. You built a little cage, put some bait in it, and then set a heavy log over the opening that was triggered when the animal walked through. The log would then fall on the animal.

It took a heck of a lot of work to build a deadfall. It

was a lot easier to just lay traps everywhere and go check them regularly.

"We'll never find anything on Surelock," Ashley grumbled after a while.

"Yeah, I know."

"I wish there was a way we could."

I thought for a second. "We could ask Miss Lily about it."

"Ah, she won't know about junk like this."

"I'll bet she'd know how to set a deadfall."

"Probably. But she won't know about something like this."

Then it occurred to me who could help. "Mr. Wilson would know for sure. Or he'd know where we could look."

Ashley nodded. "My dad says he's been around forever."

Everyone knew Mr. Wilson. He was a gruff, ornery ranger who'd seen and done everything. He knew the Sierra Nevadas almost as well as John Muir, who'd hiked every inch of the place.

"I'll ask him tomorrow, when I go to the ranger station with Mark."

"You're not going without me this time," Ashley said sternly.

"But—"

"Forget it. I'm goin' with you," she said, ending the discussion.

△
CHAPTER 8

△Sure enough, Ashley was up at the crack of dawn, knocking at my door. She was going with me. No questions asked.

Mark didn't say anything about Ashley coming along. I guess he figured there was no stopping her.

"You think Mr. Wilson can help?" Mark asked.

"We hope so," Ashley answered through a mouthful of blueberry muffin, which she quickly washed down with orange juice.

As always, I could see that Ashley would undoubtedly finish off her "second" breakfast before I was halfway through my first. She always did that.

Mark turned to me. "You know I won't be around camp much today?"

I nodded. "Yeah, I know you have to go out on that trail."

A flash flood had wiped out one of the main trails

near Mark's station, and I knew that a whole bunch of the rangers were going out to clear away a lot of the debris and re-mark the trail.

"You'll be OK by yourself?" he asked.

I just glared at him. "Yeah, of course. No problem."

"I have to ask." Mark smiled. "Your mom would kill me if I didn't."

That brought a dirty look from my mom, but she didn't say anything. I noticed she usually didn't when Mark and I were talking about junk.

"Hey!" Ashley said, practically falling out of her seat.

"What?" I asked.

"I almost forgot," she said excitedly. "I have to show you something. I found another trap."

We all did a double take. "You did?" I said.

"Yeah, it's not too far from here," Ashley said.

I pushed my chair back and grabbed the muffin I hadn't eaten yet. "Show me."

"Hey, we have to go soon," Mark said.

"We'll be back in a sec'," I told him. "Don't worry."

Mark checked his watch. "I'll give you half an hour. If you're not back, I'm takin' off."

"Got it!" I nodded. I grabbed a windbreaker I'd left hanging near the kitchen door. "Come on, Ashley, let's go."

Ashley got up from her chair. "Thanks, Mrs. Rawlings."

Mom smiled back. "Be careful, Josh."

"Sure," I grunted. I was already moving toward the door.

Ashley pushed past me and started to run. I followed quickly. "Slowpoke," she teased. She turned hard to the left once she was clear of the porch and then hard left again. She was going straight up the mountain out behind our house.

I didn't answer. I just ran to her side and matched her stride. Ashley slowed down to a fast walk. Sometimes she just drove me crazy. I think she did it on purpose.

"So where's this trap?" I asked.

"Up the mountain behind our houses, not too far from here."

"Really?"

"Yeah, and you know what? It's a steel-jaw."

I almost stopped in my tracks. "A steel-jaw trap? Near here?"

"Yeah, and it's a wicked-looking thing. It's big and ugly."

I gave Ashley a weird look. "Why didn't you say anything about this yesterday, when we were looking through the encyclopedia?"

Ashley gave me that look of hers, the one that said she thought I was a complete moron. " 'Cause I was mad at you, course. Why d' you think?"

I just shook my head. Ashley could *really* drive you crazy sometimes.

"So is it a Surelock, like the other one?"

"Don't know," she said. "When I saw it I didn't know what it was—at least, not until last night when you were telling me about that other trap, the one that caught the badger."

Ashley started to pick up the pace again. But this time I was ready. I matched her stride easily.

It took us about five minutes to get to the top of the ridge that looked out over our little community of homes on Ganymede. Ashley and I had been up here dozens of times. There were a couple of clearings up here, and one little spring where water trickled out.

"So where is it?" I asked, trying not to let Ashley see that I was winded.

"Close. It's near the spring."

"Really?" I asked, slightly incredulous. The trap must have been set recently. We'd been up here less than a week ago.

We started to work our way through the underbrush toward the spring. There wasn't quite a path to it, but we both knew where it was.

As we neared the spring, I started to get this funny feeling in the pit of my stomach. I couldn't explain it. I just felt strange, like something was wrong and I couldn't figure out what it was.

The spring was covered by a small pile of rocks, and the water usually just sort of dribbled up and out between some of the rocks and then meandered down the side of the mountain.

I knew that quite a lot of animals came and used the spring to get their water, because I'd seen all kinds of tracks up here. I'd spotted the tracks of opossum, deer, fox, rabbits, raccoon, even an occasional bobcat.

"The trap's up above the spring," Ashley whispered as we drew near it.

We came to the clearing. There was nothing unusual, it seemed. Everything was quiet.

We walked through the clearing. The spring was

bubbling and gurgling happily. There had been a heavy rain recently, and there was more water than usual coming up.

Ashley marched right up to where she remembered the trap was. Then she stopped in her tracks. She covered her mouth and stifled a scream. I saw it at almost the same time. There was a raccoon caught in the trap.

The raccoon was lying on its side, one of its feet caught in the steel jaws of the trap. It wasn't moving at all. Its fur was a tangled mat from its furious struggle to free itself.

I immediately thought of the badger. The raccoon had obviously been too weak from its own struggle, or it might have tried to get out as the badger had.

There was so much fur, mud, and blood around, you almost couldn't tell it was a raccoon. The underbrush was completely trampled around the trap. At the edge, I spotted a strange set of tracks that almost looked like those of bare, human feet not much bigger than mine. But that made no sense. Plus, more gym shoe tracks about the size of my own.

"We should do something," Ashley said, the pain obvious in her voice.

"What? It's probably dead."

Ashley took a step closer. I did too. We both looked hard to see if it was breathing. I couldn't tell.

I looked around for a long stick. There was one way to check. When I'd found one that was suitable, I grabbed it and reached out.

"Don't hurt it," Ashley pleaded.

"I won't," I growled back. "Relax. I just wanna see if it's alive."

I positioned the stick and inched it beneath the belly of the raccoon. There was no movement. But the raccoon wasn't stiff, either, like it would be if it was dead. It was soft, and the stick pushed against the body.

When I lifted the stick a little, there was the slightest bit of movement. The raccoon was alive, but just barely.

"It's alive," I said.

"I can see that."

"So what do we do now?"

"We have to free it, of course."

I frowned. "Even if we do, it'll never live. Not the way it is."

"Then let's take it with us."

"Just carry it down to the house?" I asked, my eyes wide.

"Yeah, sure. Why not?"

"And who's gonna look after it?"

Ashley's eyes twinkled mischievously. "You are."

I sighed. "Mom would kill me."

"Not when she sees it, she won't."

I looked back at the motionless raccoon. I knew it was hopeless, trying to help the creature. Better to just put it out of its misery. But I also knew Ashley would never sit still for that.

"OK, so how do we get it down the mountain?" I asked glumly.

"Carry it."

"With what?"

Ashley reached over and gave me a playful shove. "Take your jacket off."

"Now, wait a minute—"

"Just put the raccoon on the top," Ashley said. "It'll wash off. Don't worry so much."

I held onto my jacket. This seemed crazy. But I also knew I'd go through with it. I had no choice, really.

"Hurry, Josh," Ashley insisted.

Reluctantly, I slipped out of the windbreaker. I knelt down and looked at the raccoon more closely. There seemed little chance that the raccoon would suddenly get up and charge me. Its breathing was quite shallow.

Still, just to be on the safe side, I put the windbreaker over it and then waited for a second. When the raccoon didn't respond, I hurried over to where the trap was staked to the ground and scrabbled at the dirt quickly. After a few hard tugs, the stake came free.

I gathered up the raccoon and the trap together in one bundle. The raccoon wasn't moving. I was ready to drop it like a hot potato at the first sign of movement, but it was clear that the raccoon wasn't going anywhere.

Ashley came over to help carry the raccoon, but it was actually easier to carry it myself. I just waved her off and tightened my grip around the raccoon. The animal was completely limp, and I had to kind of gather it all up in order to carry it.

Ashley led the way down the mountain. She picked a route that was mostly clear of trees and boulders, so I wouldn't have to worry too much about where I was going.

I only stumbled once, but it was enough to give me quite a fright. A picture flashed through my mind, of me pitching headlong and burying my face into the half-dead raccoon. But I recovered quickly, and I didn't stumble again.

As I walked, another thought also occurred to me. There was no way to know for sure, but this could be the same raccoon I'd been feeding dinner scraps to from my back porch almost from the time I'd moved to the Sierra Nevadas.

It had taken me forever to learn just what a raccoon would eat and what it wouldn't. Mostly I learned from trial and error. I'd put things out, and the raccoon would leave some stuff untouched and completely devour other things.

The raccoon hated oily, fatty stuff. But it also didn't like the dried-out foods, either. It was an especially picky, finicky eater.

This could be that raccoon. I'd never seen it in the daylight, but this was pretty close to our house, right behind it and up the mountain.

In fact, the more I thought about it, the more likely it seemed that this was the very same raccoon. And it made me sad. Most likely, I wouldn't have the chance to play those night games with it anymore.

"Should we tell my mom?" I asked as we drew closer to my house.

"No," Ashley whispered. "Let's just take it out to your little shed first."

There was a shed out behind our log house. We didn't use it much. Mostly, it just stored a beat-up lawn mower, some hedge clippers, and other things for yard work.

Ashley opened the door and pulled the light switch. She cleared away some of the stuff on the floor to make space for the raccoon. I laid it down gently. The animal hadn't moved the entire trip down the mountain.

We both knelt down beside it. Ashley opened the coat carefully. The pitiful creature looked even worse here in the dim light of the shed. It had blood caked in its eyes, and there was mud caked under its stomach.

"We need some warm water and soap," Ashley said in a soft voice. "We have to clean its wounds."

"You go get some. I'll try to get the trap off."

"Be careful. Don't hurt it."

I frowned. "I don't think there's much more we can do to it."

"Just be careful."

I didn't answer. Ashley got up and left. I picked up the stake and turned it over in my hand. It was exactly like the other one, the stake that had been attached to the trap that had gotten the badger.

I was tempted to look at the trap itself to see if it was a Surelock, like the other one. But I had to free the raccoon first.

I grabbed both sides of the steel jaws and pulled. It wouldn't open. I pulled even harder. It still wouldn't open. "Man," I muttered to myself. "No wonder the raccoon couldn't get loose."

This trap clearly had been made to keep an animal trapped for good. I reached over and grabbed the heavy, rust-encrusted stake and wedged the flat end between the two steel jaws of the trap. Then I pried the trap open.

When the jaws were an inch or so apart, I moved the trap slightly. The raccoon's paw slipped free.

I dropped the stake and moved closer to look at the raccoon's paw. The thing was obviously crushed. Even if the animal lived, I seriously doubted if it would ever walk again without a pretty severe limp.

But I guess it didn't matter too much to a trapper whether an animal caught in one of these traps ever walked again, or what kind of suffering it went through once it was trapped. As long as the animal couldn't get free, and its hide was intact, that was all that mattered.

"Poor thing," I said gently, picking up the limp paw of the still creature. The breathing was even shallower. I wasn't sure, really, what to do now. I had no idea how you were supposed to bring a near-dead raccoon back to life.

Ashley came back through the door. I looked up. A little shiver of surprise went through me. My mom was standing next to her. She was carrying a little bucket. I could hear the water sloshing inside.

"Let me take a look," Mom said firmly.

I moved to one side and let Mom kneel down beside the raccoon. "I just took the trap off," I said.

Mom was grim-faced. I could see this troubled her as much as it did me. She took one look at the trap and then turned her attention to the raccoon. She dipped the rag in the water and applied it gently to the most obvious wounds from the struggle.

It took Mom about five minutes to clean the raccoon. Neither Ashley nor I said anything during the entire time she was working. The animal didn't respond.

When Mom was finished, she stood up stiffly. She looked over at Ashley. "I'll come in with you and find an old box and a blanket," she said. "You can bring it out here and set it up in the corner. You'll need to wrap the raccoon up in it."

Ashley nodded. "Do . . . um, do you think it's gonna live?"

Mom shook her head. "Honestly? No, I don't."

"But we have to try, don't we?" I said.

Mom looked back at me. "Sure, Josh. Give it your best shot. But don't be disappointed if it doesn't work. Most likely, this raccoon won't survive the next twenty-four hours."

After Mom and Ashley had left, I finally reached out and turned the trap over. It was a Surelock. It was the same kind of trap—ancient and heavy. The trapper sure was covering a wide territory.

More than ever, now, I was determined to figure out what was going on. Why was this trapper around here, so close to some of the big national parks? Why was he so close to where all the rangers would find him? I couldn't figure it.

The whole thing made no sense. Why was someone going around and laying all of these ancient traps? Did someone really want the furs so badly that they'd risk getting caught by the rangers if they happened to trap an endangered animal?

I didn't have any answers. Maybe there weren't any. But I was sure going to try to find them.

Mom and Ashley returned with a box and an old blanket. They set it up in the corner. Then I moved the raccoon over to the box. I carried it in my windbreaker. Once it was safely nestled in the blanket, I pulled my jacket free. Ashley covered the creature up with the blanket.

"Go. Mark's waiting," Mom ordered. "There's nothing more you can do for it now. It needs to rest for the rest of the day."

"But—" I began to protest.

"There's nothing more you can do," Mom said firmly. "Trust me. It will sleep for the rest of the day. Either that, or it won't make it."

I looked over at Ashley. She just shrugged. "Not much we can do now, I guess."

I took one last look at the raccoon half-buried by the blanket. I hated to leave it. But I knew my mom was right. I just had to wait and see what happened.

"All right," I sighed. "Let's go. But, Mom, call me at the station if anything happens. OK?"

Mom smiled wanly. "It's a deal. Now get moving."

△
CHAPTER 9

△Mr. Wilson was pretty casual about it all. He thought we were wasting our time, trying to save the raccoon.

"Be better off if you just shot it," Mr. Wilson said gruffly.

"No!" Ashley said quickly.

"Little missy, I'm not being mean," Mr. Wilson said more gently, turning his attention to Ashley. "But that raccoon would be better off if you just put it out of its misery right now."

"We're gonna try," Ashley said.

Ashley and I were helping Mr. Wilson out along a well-marked trail near the ranger station. Mark had gone off with a bunch of the other rangers to keep working on the trail that had been washed out by a flash flood. We were working our way along a trail closer to home.

Mr. Wilson was an interesting guy. Sometimes he didn't say much at all. He'd go along for a while, and then he'd just come out with something. Like today.

"That trapper's an old-timer," he declared about mid-morning.

"A what?" I asked him.

"An old-timer," he repeated.

"What's that mean, exactly?" Ashley asked.

"I mean he's from the old school of trapping, where you didn't worry a whole lot about how you got the animal," Mr. Wilson said. "You just got it, period. You killed the animal by hook or by crook. Never mind how you did it."

"There's a better way?" I asked.

"Yeah, sure." Mr. Wilson shrugged. "At least, there are more humane ways. You can kill animals these days without putting them through all that nonsense."

"Really?" Ashley asked.

"You know," Mr. Wilson sighed, "I wouldn't be a bit surprised if we didn't see a huge bear trap or two show up, this trapper's using stuff that's so old."

"A bear trap? What's that?" I asked.

Mr. Wilson stood up. He'd been laying a little yellow marker ribbon along a tree stump at the side of the trail. This particular trail was a very well-worn path, the kind of path families took with their young children. It wasn't at all like the trails that wound their way through the other parts of the Sierra Nevadas, where you didn't have many markers to guide you.

"A bear trap," Mr. Wilson said slowly, "is a huge

monstrosity. The thing weighs about thirty pounds. It would crush the bear's leg when it was sprung. You can see them in museums these days."

"In museums?" I asked.

"Yeah, or sometimes farmers will stick an old bear trap up on the back of their barns out in the backcountry," Mr. Wilson said. "There's a guy west of Jupiter—at the old Keenan place—who's had one up on the back of his barn for thirty, forty years."

"The Keenan place?" I asked.

"Yeah, ole Keenan," Mr. Wilson mused. "Think he had all sorts of old traps there once, to go along with his prize bear trap that he never used, best as I can remember."

"I think I've seen one of those before," Ashley said.

"When I first became a ranger back in 1961—before both of you were born—some of the states were just starting to outlaw those bear traps," Mr. Wilson continued.

"They were that dangerous?" Ashley asked.

"Yep, they were," he said, nodding. "Then this guy named Jack Aldrich came along and figured out a better way to catch a bear. He made a legsnare that had a noose and a very flexible steel cable. All the other traps started to look more like that trap, and the huge bear traps started to disappear. Today, you couldn't find one except, like I said, in a museum or on the back of a barn."

"But this trapper who caught the raccoon, you think he's using old traps?" I asked.

"That steel-jaw, the one that got the badger—and

71

it sounds like what got your raccoon—is an old, old design. I haven't seen one like it in years. Not since I first became a ranger."

Ashley and I didn't say anything. It all still made no sense to me, really. I couldn't figure out what was happening.

We moved along the trail. It was a wide trail, with plenty of room to walk. It was so well trampled, I didn't even bother to check for animal tracks. There wouldn't be any on a path like this. It was a human trail. Animals would avoid it completely.

"You ever heard of a Surelock?" I asked Mr. Wilson.

He shook his head. "Nope. It's not a design I can recall hearing about. Course it could have been real popular once. Like back in the fifties, maybe. Just don't know."

"Is there a way to find out?" Ashley asked.

"Not that I know of," he grunted. "Guess you could ask around. Don't know what else you could try."

"Who should I ask?" Ashley said.

"Me," Mr. Wilson laughed. "And I don't know. You could also go into Jupiter and ask the Checkers Gang."

I looked over at Ashley. She was nodding, like she knew exactly what Mr. Wilson was talking about. I hated it when people knew stuff that I didn't have a clue about.

"The Checkers Gang?" I demanded.

"You don't know who they are?" Ashley asked playfully.

"No, I don't," I snapped.

"They sit out on the front porch of the big general store in the middle of Jupiter," offered Mr. Wilson.

"The old guys," Ashley said bluntly. "They sit out there and play checkers, practically all the time. You can almost always see them out there. There's four of 'em."

"Yeah, old guys, like me," Mr. Wilson chuckled.

"I didn't mean it like that," Ashley said quickly.

"Yes, you did," he laughed. "But don't worry. I'm not offended. It's true. They're four old guys who sit on the porch and play checkers, rain or shine."

"The Checkers Gang," I said, shaking my head. I had some vague recollection of a big front porch at the General Store and people sitting in chairs on it. But not much more than that. "They really do that?"

"They sure do," Mr. Wilson said. "And they've been around the block, so to speak. I'd ask one of them if they've heard about this Surelock trap design. They might have."

Ashley nodded. "Yeah, it's worth a shot."

"All right," I said. "We'll do just that."

Mr. Wilson suddenly looked over at me. "You're going out with your stepdad soon, aren't you?"

"Two days," I said, nodding. "We've got it all planned."

"Where you headed?" Mr. Wilson asked.

"Sabertooth Pass, and then Ghost Canyon," I said.

Mr. Wilson nodded. "Yeah, that's right. Mark was checking on the snow conditions. You can get through that pass right now?"

"Yeah, Mark says so," I told him.

"Well, be careful, OK?"

"I will," I promised. "Don't worry about us. We'll be fine."

△
CHAPTER 10

△The Checkers Gang was there, right where Mr. Wilson said they'd be. They were always there, it seemed. First thing in the morning, at lunch, dinner, until it got too dark to see the faded checkers anymore.

It turned out they didn't just play checkers. Good thing, I figured. Who could play checkers all day, every day?

No, the Checkers Gang played checkers only occasionally, when they weren't being deadly serious. At other times, they played chess, or backgammon, or a whole bunch of different card games.

But they were always right there on that front porch of the General Store in downtown Jupiter.

Jupiter was a pretty small town. Nothing like Washington, D.C., where I'd grown up and where we'd moved from the past spring.

Jupiter was small enough that you could stand at one end of the main street and pretty much see the other end of town from where you stood. It was a straight shot, from one end of that street to the other. The main street was called Main Street.

There were stores for most of the things you needed—one store for clothes, another for food, a third for hardware, a fourth for junk you needed around the house.

The General Store, though, had a little bit of everything. That's probably why it was the hangout.

Because, it seemed, the General Store wasn't just the place where the Checkers Gang hung out. It was also where some of the kids who lived in or near Jupiter itself always hung out.

Ashley and I didn't see kids from Jupiter much. We'd see them when I started school in the fall, of course. But because Ganymede was about fifteen miles away, and because Ashley and I tended to spend most of our time out in the wilderness or in the woods around our community of homes, I hadn't met kids from Jupiter.

Ashley's dad had been going into Jupiter anyway, so we hitched a ride with him. He dropped us off at the General Store while he ran his errands.

"Be careful," Ashley's dad said to us as we scrambled to get out of his car.

"Don't worry, Dad," Ashley reassured him.

"I'll swing back by in an hour," he said. "You'll be outside?"

"Right here," she said, and slammed the car door shut.

We both turned and faced the General Store. The

Checkers Gang was there, sitting in their rocking chairs on the front porch, leaning over some kind of a game board.

There were also six kids—five boys and one girl—outside the store. Two of them were probably two or three years older than Ashley and me. The others were maybe our age, or a little younger.

They were all just sitting on the top step of the General Store. They each had a pile of stones on one side, and a pile of pennies on the other.

Maybe twenty feet in front of them, at the edge of the street, was a tin can. There were stones and pebbles scattered all around the tin can, which was sitting open-end-up.

"Awright, *go!*" said one of the two older boys, who had a quite faded blue and white striped hat pulled down low over his forehead.

Everyone fired a pebble at the tin can. Five of them missed entirely. The sixth hit the can, but the stone plinked off and fell to one side.

"Crud!" the kid muttered. "Had it right there."

"Weren't even close," one of the older boys jeered.

"You blind?" the first kid said. "It hit the top."

"Nah," the older kid laughed. "It skipped into it."

"No way, it—"

"Awright, *go!*" the other older boy said loudly, interrupting the fight.

The other kids fired another round of pebbles at the tin can. This time, all six landed a few inches from the can and rolled harmlessly past it.

"We *gotta* move it closer," one of the kids complained.

"Yeah, we ain't even comin' nowheres close," a second groused.

The girl, who wore a dress that was patched in at least four places and whose hair was matted and tangled in so many places I couldn't even tell how long it was, stood up. She started to walk toward the tin can. I noticed that she wasn't wearing shoes, which seemed to fit with her raggedy outfit.

"Don't you touch it!" one of the older boys barked.

The girl turned and planted her hands squarely on her hips. "Aw, get off it, Shawn. You gotta move it in. We ain't got near the thing for hours."

"Don't move it!" the boy said again.

The girl turned anyway and walked up to the can. She picked it up and moved it five feet closer. Then she walked back.

The older boy who'd ordered her not to touch it just glared at her. But he didn't say anything. He just grabbed another pebble and waited for the command to fire.

Ashley and I looked at each other. I wasn't exactly sure what was going on here, but after the next round, it became more clear.

This time, one of the younger boys actually sank his pebble in the can. He let out a wild, exuberant shout as he did so.

"Yeah! Gimme that money," he demanded, turning to face the others. " 'Member, it was a three-penny."

"Ain't no way that was a three-penny," the older boy who'd complained said. "Rachel moved it closer. I figure it was worth just a penny."

"Uh, no way!" bellowed the kid who'd made the

shot. "We agreed. It was a three-penny. Can't change the rules now. And you *got* the money. I know. Your granddad just nabbed another—"

One of the older boys reached out and smacked the kid real hard. It almost knocked the kid over. "Shut up, you moron," the older kid barked.

"Hey, I just meant—"

"I know what you meant. But you got no say in any of this."

"I let you bust up my old guitar so's that your granddad—"

The older kid smacked him again. Even harder. "We'll give you one penny. That's it."

"You can't change the rules," the kid whined, even as he tilted his head to one side, cradling the side where he'd been whacked.

"Can too!" The older kid grinned. "I'm doin' it now."

The kid's exuberant smile was beginning to droop a little. He faced the other kids. "Fork over," he said, not quite as confidently.

"One penny," another kid said.

The girl, Rachel, stood up again. "I moved the can," she declared. "So we'll split it. A two-penny."

That seemed to meet with universal agreement—except, of course, with the kid who was expecting three pennies from everyone.

I finally had the game figured out. They were firing at the tin cup, after having agreed on just how much it was worth if you sank the shot in the tin can. I figured they played for more pennies the farther the tin cup was from the porch.

Rachel was the first to notice Ashley and me

standing awkwardly off to one side. She looked over at us after she'd handed her two pennies to the kid who'd made the shot.

"Whatcha gawkin' at?" she scowled.

I looked down. Ashley just stared back at the girl. "Nothing," Ashley said, tight-lipped. "We were going to the store."

"Well, move it, Ash-heap," Rachel taunted. "I tole ya to stay outta my way, and I meant it."

"I'm not in your way," Ashley said, her voice edged with more anger than I'd ever heard.

Something was going on here, something I couldn't understand. Probably something I would only learn over time.

Ashley and this girl Rachel had clearly had a run-in somewhere, at some time. It was etched on both of their faces.

"Ya better not be," Rachel warned. "I'll take ya out."

Ashley didn't answer. I could see that she was torn between just walking on, or maybe going over to tangle with this wild girl. I wasn't sure which path made more sense.

"Look, it's cool," I said, my voice dry and raspy.

"Who're you?" one of the older boys demanded.

"I, um, I just moved here," I said. "My stepdad's a ranger out at—"

"One of the Rudy Ranger boys!" a boy yelled. "You gonna arrest us for trespassin'?"

"Yeah, we heard 'bout you," the boy Shawn said.

"You have?" I asked, surprised.

Shawn nodded. "We know where *all* the ranger boys are. We got 'em all covered."

80

Ashley reached over and tugged on my sleeve. "Let's go," she whispered fiercely, loud enough so only I could hear.

I wanted to stay. I really did. I was genuinely curious about this crowd, who they were, why they were so hostile to us. But I could see that Ashley was also very anxious to move on. So I followed her lead.

"That's it, move it on," Rachel called out after us as we began to walk up the steps that led to the General Store and then down toward the end of the long porch where the Checkers Gang sat.

Ashley ignored the last taunt and kept walking. I did too. But when we were out of earshot, I just had to ask.

I leaned close to her. "What in the—?"

"Trash," she said through gritted teeth. "Big-time trash."

"What do you mean?"

"You'll see, when you start school. Shawn and the other boy, Dunk—for Duncan—are in our school. They'll be in ninth, two years ahead of us."

"That girl, Rachel? Is she our age?"

Ashley nodded. "Unfortunately. She'll also be in seventh."

"So what's the deal, anyway?"

Ashley risked a glance over her shoulder. The kids were back into their little game. I heard a *plink* as a pebble bounced off the tin can. "Rachel and I don't exactly get along," she said wryly.

"Yeah, I can see that. But why?"

"A long story." Ashley grimaced. "I'll tell it to you sometime. Not now."

"Come on. Just tell me."

Ashley sighed. "All right. Real quick. She thought I stole her boyfriend away."

"Did you?" Somehow the thought of Ashley stealing any boy away from someone else didn't add up. I suppose it was possible. It just didn't seem likely.

"You kiddin'?" Ashley laughed. "No way would I ever come near anybody she was around. No way. Not ever."

"So how did she think that?"

"Her dumb boyfriend liked me, I think. And he told her that. Then she got mad. We got in this huge monster fight. We both almost got kicked out of school."

"So who won the fight?"

Ashley smiled viciously. "I stomped her. They had to pull me off her."

I looked back again. That would be a whale of a fight, Ashley against that wild girl. I didn't doubt for a second that Ashley could stomp her. But that girl was pretty formidable. I wasn't sure I'd want to tangle with her.

"You said they were trash," I said quietly. "What's that mean, anyway?"

Ashley looked really uncomfortable. "Dad says I shouldn't talk like that, that people are good, really, and that I shouldn't hold it against her because . . . because . . ." Ashley looked away.

"Because what?"

"Because her mom ran away with some high school guy, because she lives out on the other side of some railroad tracks out in the middle of the woods with her great-grandfather, her grandpa, her dad, and her two uncles and because, well . . ."

"What?" I asked. This all seemed so bizarre to me. Who was this girl, anyway?

Ashley turned and looked at me directly. "Look. Just forget it. I don't like her. That's all. She tried to beat me up, we got in this huge fight, and that's all there is to it. OK? Can we just drop it?"

I didn't want to forget it. Something was going on here, something I most definitely did not understand. But I didn't want to push. Ashley was obviously having a great deal of trouble with it. So I decided to wait.

"OK." I nodded. "Let's go talk to the Checkers Gang."

Relieved, Ashley moved quickly down the porch. I followed. I could still hear the raucous shouts of Rachel and the others, though, as I walked away.

The Checkers Gang was in the middle of two backgammon games when we arrived. I'd only played backgammon a couple of times, but I could tell that the games were just about over because the players only had a couple of pieces left on the board.

Ashley and I stood off to the side and watched for a few moments. None of the members of the Gang looked up, really. One of them glanced at me, gave me a quick smile, and then returned to the game. These were serious players.

All four men looked remarkably similar, almost as if they could be brothers. All four had whitish-gray hair, which was covered by a cap of some sort. All of them wore long plaid pants, even though it was summer, and a knit shirt. All of them had soft-soled shoes of some kind.

When the first two finished their game, the loser

reached out across the board and offered his hand. The winner took it, gave it a quick shake, and then they finally turned to us.

"Haven't had any spectators in a while," the first said to Ashley with a kind smile. "You *are* here to watch our matches, right?"

Before Ashley could respond, his playing partner chuckled. "We charge admission, you know."

Ashley and I both started. "Admission?" I asked blankly.

"Sure, of course," the first said. "You didn't know?"

"Um, no, I guess we didn't," I grimaced.

"You need intellectual capital," the second said. "You have any of that?"

"Intellectual capital?" I asked. "What's that?"

The two men laughed. "Just a joke, son," said the first. "Intellectual capital means your smarts, what you know, what you've learned. When you talk, you have to spend a little of it. That's what we buy and sell around here. Good talk. That's all."

I nodded. I wasn't exactly sure I had these guys figured out. But I also knew they seemed pretty harmless.

The first player looked at Ashley. "You've been here before. Right?" Ashley nodded. "But the other one, your friend, he's new?"

"I've been here a couple of months," I said quickly.

"Couple of months." The first player smiled. "I'd say that's new."

The second player nodded at me. "Name's Willis. My partner's name is Gradison. We call him Graddy. Over there, that's Doc and Sid."

Doc and Sid looked up briefly, and then returned to their game. Like I said, these were *serious* players.

"You two look like you're on a mission," Graddy said with a smile.

I couldn't help it, really. I liked these guys. I had absolutely nothing whatsoever in common with them. But I liked them. They were happy and harmless.

"We are," Ashley answered. "One of the rangers said you might be able to help us."

"One of the rangers?" Willis asked. "That'd be ole Wilson, most likely. Right?"

I nodded. "Yeah, but how . . . ?"

Graddy and Willis laughed, almost as if on cue. "Wilson sends folks our way every time he's stumped, that's why. So he must have run across something he couldn't figure. That about right?"

"Well, actually, yeah, it is," Ashley said.

"So what can we do for you, little lady?" Graddy leaned back in his chair and tipped his hat back slightly.

Ashley jumped right in. "We're trying to figure something out. Somebody's been layin' traps, real close to where people live. They're steel-jaw traps. One of 'em got Josh's pet raccoon the other day—"

"It wasn't exactly a pet," I interrupted.

"But you were feeding it," Ashley said, moving on quickly. "So it was like a pet." I didn't say anything more to correct her. I guess it was close enough to the truth. "Anyway, it got caught in this steel-jaw trap. And it wasn't the first time."

"The first time?" Graddy asked.

"The first time we've come across one of these steel-jaw traps," Ashley said.

"They're plenty of steel-jaws around," Willis mused.

"Yeah, but this one's real old," Ashley said.

"How old?" asked Graddy.

"All rusted out," I said.

"And held in place with this big, hairy spike of some sort," Ashley said.

"Like a railroad spike," I said.

"And the name on the back of the trap was 'Surelock,'" Ashley continued. "Mr. Wilson's never heard of it, and neither has my dad. Or Josh's stepdad. They're both rangers."

Willis and Graddy nodded as one. They exchanged glances. Neither said anything right away.

Finally, Graddy looked over at the other two players. "Hey, Sid, whatcha know about a Surelock? Anything?"

Sid looked up from his game briefly. "He had a sidekick named Watson." Then Sid looked back down at his game.

"No, not Holmes," Graddy said with a frown. "A Surelock trap. A steel-jaw."

Sid didn't even look up from his game. "There aren't any Surelocks around. Haven't been for forty, forty-five years, at least."

"Forty years!" I exclaimed.

"You deaf, boy?" Sid said, still without looking up from his game. "They went outta business back in 1948, after the war."

"And have you heard about people using them, that kind of trap?" Ashley called out.

"Haven't seen or heard about a Surelock since, oh, I think maybe 1952 or thereabouts," Sid said. "But don't hold me to the year. My memory's not what it used to be."

"Never was much to begin with," Doc grumbled, also without looking up.

"Better'n yours was," Sid said.

"I've forgotten more than you ever knew," Doc countered.

"First part's true, about how much you've forgotten," Sid said.

Doc just glowered, and then rolled the dice. A big number came up and Doc moved his pieces. "Take that."

I looked back at Graddy. "The company that made Surelocks went out of business in 1948?"

Graddy nodded. "If Sid says so, believe it. Sid knows his stuff, especially about things like that. He knows it backwards and forwards. He's been here longer than all the rest of us, and he knows this country like the back of his hand."

"And if he says he hasn't seen that kind of trap for forty or forty-five years—" Ashley began.

"Then you can believe it," Graddy said, nodding. "Sid would know."

I looked over at the two of them. They were still completely and totally absorbed in their game. "They always like that?" I asked.

"Just about," Graddy laughed. "They take the game just a mite more serious than either Willis or I do."

Ashley and I hung around for about another fifteen minutes or so. Graddy and Willis started a card game.

They were nice enough to ask us if we wanted to join them. But Ashley and I could see they didn't really mean it. They were only saying it to be polite.

But they didn't seem to mind that we hung around. And I sure didn't want to go back where Rachel and the boys were still pitching pebbles. It seemed a whole lot safer on this end of the porch.

Just before we left, when Ashley's dad drove up, Graddy gave us one last bit of advice.

"Stay clear of those ones," Graddy warned.

"Which ones?" I asked, slightly confused by what he meant.

"Those," Graddy said, pointing directly at Rachel and her friends.

"Rachel and Shawn and Dunk?" asked Ashley.

Graddy nodded grimly. "They'll land in big-time trouble one of these days. They've been trouble ever since their grandad got laid off from the railroad back in my day and took to the woods. You'd do well to steer clear of them. Just a little friendly advice."

△
CHAPTER 11

△I felt like a mule. Or at least I had some idea what a mule felt like. No wonder they balked so much. It was a lousy job, being a beast of burden.

Mark had me so loaded down with stuff on my backpack I felt like I could barely move and breathe.

"You'll get used to it," Mark had laughed. "Don't worry."

Don't worry. Yeah, right. It felt like I was carrying a house on my back. The backpack I was going to carry into the wilderness with me was just about as tall as me. It was filled with several changes of clothes, enough food for a week, a bedroll, and my sleeping bag. Mark was carrying the tent with his pack.

I wished there was an easier way. But I knew there wasn't. You had to go into the wilderness prepared for the worst, which meant you had to take more stuff with you than you would if you were just going out for a picnic or something.

Like warm clothes. Mark insisted we take some with us, even though it was now pretty hot during the day. You never knew, he'd said. It got cold at night, plus we'd come into a little snow around the edges of the pass, most likely.

It seemed wild to me that we'd actually find snow now, at this time of year. But Mark knew what he was talking about. If he said there would be snow, then there would be snow.

We were going to drive to the Hopewell ranger station first thing Saturday morning. Our packs were already stowed in the back of Mark's car, so we just had to get up, grab something to eat and then take off.

I was surprised to see that Mom got up, too. She was waiting for us in the kitchen. There were some eggs and bacon and muffins. She'd probably been up for at least half an hour.

"You *will* be careful, won't you, Josh?" she asked me.

I looked up with a mouthful of eggs. I waited for a second as I swallowed. "You know, you say that to me practically every time I leave the house."

"And I mean it. You need to be reminded."

"*All* the time?"

"All the time." Mom smiled. "Somebody has to look after you. Might as well be me."

"But I am careful."

"Well, be especially careful this time," Mom said somberly. "This isn't a Sunday stroll in the park."

"Mom!" I said, exasperated. "Mark knows what he's doing. We'll be fine."

"I just worry," Mom said softly. "You know me."

Mark held up a hand. "We'll be careful, I promise. Now, Josh, let's roll."

I scooted my chair back. Mom reached over and gave my arm an affectionate squeeze. I hated mushy junk like that, but I knew I didn't have much choice. People, especially moms, gave hugs and kisses all the time. You just had to put up with it.

"Hey, Mom, you'll look after the raccoon, right?"

Mom smiled. "Don't worry, kid. I've got it all under control. That raccoon's going to be just fine."

The raccoon had made it through the night and the next day, thanks to several stints of bottle feeding from me and Ashley and Mom. It was clearly getting stronger. The foot would never be the same. But I was sure it would live now.

The raccoon didn't move much. Just enough to take the bottle and guzzle the warm milk inside. It didn't seem afraid, really. A little dazed at all that had happened to it, but that was about it.

"Great. Thanks, Mom. You're great," I said.

"I know," she said.

"Well, I'll see ya then," I said quickly, turning to hurry from the kitchen before anything else much could happen. "We'll be careful."

"Promise?"

I nodded. "Yep, no problem."

Mark and I escaped without further harm. When we were safely in the car and on our way, Mark just started laughing softly to himself for no reason.

"What's so funny?" I demanded.

"You."

"Whatcha mean?"

"Oh, when your mom tells you to be careful. You get so mad."

"I wasn't mad, exactly."

"Bent out of shape, then."

"It's just that she doesn't need to tell me."

"She has to, Josh. It's what moms do."

I sighed. "I know. But it still drives me nuts."

It was still dark when we left, but it was an easy drive to the Hopewell station. Basically, we followed the main road that ran alongside the Hialeah River, and then took a left onto a narrow road that led to the ranger station.

We passed through the Giant Forest on the way. I could see the huge redwoods standing silent guard just off the road, towering well above us, blocking out the sun's rays just peeking up over the horizon.

Mark stopped the car so we could take a look at them. They went up and up and up, until I couldn't look any higher. How could a tree be so big? They were like mountains.

Mark said we wouldn't be walking through any big redwood stands. The really huge redwood meadow was north of where we were going to hike, but there would still be a few big trees along the trail we were hiking.

I was in awe of the redwoods. There was no way around it. They were *so* big. How could anything be that large, and still be alive? They seemed to go on forever.

There was just one ranger at Hopewell, and he came out to greet us as we pulled in. Hopewell was tiny, just an outpost really. There was usually just one Forest Service ranger stationed there, to keep track of things.

"Greetings!" boomed the ranger as we emerged from the car.

"Howdy," Mark answered back. I just waved.

The ranger came around the rear of the car and held the back open as we got our packs. "You gonna carry all that?" he asked me, eyeing the pack I'd be toting.

I jerked my thumb at Mark. "I tried to tell him I'd never make it."

"You'll be fine," Mark laughed. "Quit complainin'."

Mark grabbed his pack and hoisted it up over his shoulders. I did the same, with the ranger's help. I was already tired and we hadn't even begun.

"One word of caution," the ranger said just before we left the station to head into the woods.

"What's that?" Mark asked.

"We've taken a couple of soundings through Sabertooth Pass in the last couple of days," the ranger said, "and we're still just a little concerned about avalanches. So watch yourself."

"Got it." Mark nodded. "We'll tread softly."

The ranger hesitated for a moment. "There's one other thing."

"Yeah?" Mark asked.

"Well," the ranger said slowly, "we've heard reports of a wolf pack on the prowl."

"Really? This far south?"

"Not confirmed," the ranger said. "Just a quick

sighting from the air, by a weather plane. But he was pretty sure of what he saw."

"We'll keep our eyes peeled," Mark said soberly. "I promise."

The ranger nodded and then headed back into his station. We went in the other direction, toward the beginning of the lightly marked trail that led south and east from the station.

I adjusted the pack on my back. I had a feeling I'd be doing that a lot, until I'd gotten it broken in. Or until it broke me.

Mark had made me rub some oil on my back before we'd left, just to make sure the pack didn't rub me raw and give me blisters. It felt a little weird, but if it meant that I wouldn't get sore, then I'd put up with it.

The trail we were hiking wasn't exactly marked with neon lights and signs. Every so often, there would be a yellow ribbon tied discreetly to a tree limb to let us know we were still on the right path, but that was about it.

Not that we needed the trail. Mark had his compass, and I had one, too. Plus, Mark had his topography maps. We could hike cross-country, if we had to. So I wasn't too worried.

We were heading to King Lakes first. We'd have to climb for most of the day, Mark had said. We'd camp at one of the lakes' edges that evening. The next morning, we'd head out for the Pass and Sabertooth Peak.

To start with, we were hiking up a trail that ran alongside a tributary that flowed from King Lakes.

Part of me wished we'd chosen an easier way to

start a hike. Why were we climbing right from the start? But another part of me didn't mind. The way I had it figured, if we spent the first day and a half climbing up to twelve thousand feet, I'd be in shape in no time. Or I'd be dead.

I let Mark lead the way. He kept an easy, steady pace. We both grabbed walking sticks early on. I had no idea if it made it any easier, but it sure didn't hurt.

The trail was pretty dark as we set off. But it got gradually lighter during that first hour, especially as my eyes adjusted.

There were wild flowers everywhere, of all colors and shapes and sizes. Mark tried to point out as many of them as he could remember as we walked, without really slowing down too much to look at them.

We came to our first garden meadow about an hour into our walk. We had just come up a sharp ridge, where we almost had to walk leaning forward, and then we dipped down slightly into an open meadow.

The colors leaped out at you, even in the summer. I knew that these wild flowers were more colorful in the spring, when they first came up, and in the fall, when the leaves changed. But now was nice, too.

The first things I saw were these tall flowering plants with boat-shaped leaves that were about a foot long and a foot wide. There were other flowers in the tall grasses just off to either side of our little path.

"Hey, Mark," I called out. "Do you know what any of these flowers are?"

Mark shook his head. "I'm not an expert on any of this stuff. I know a little, I guess."

I pointed at one of the boat leaves. "What's this?"

95

"A leaf." Mark grinned. "Right?"

I looked around. He was obviously no help. I saw another plant that was yellow and gold, with five spurred petals. There were tons of these all around. "You know what this is?"

"Yep."

"So what is it already?"

"It's columbine."

"Yeah?" I looked down at the spurred petals. So this was columbine. I'd never heard of it.

I ran across another, quite similar blue-and-white flower with spurred petals. "And this?"

"It's a larkspur," Mark called out.

"I thought you said you didn't know anything about flowers?"

"I don't."

Another one had a branch with long, rounded petals toward the middle of the branch, and a bunch of shorter double petals at the top. I showed it to Mark. "What's this?"

Mark pursed his lips. "When a wolf howls . . ."

"What?" I asked, confused.

"Lupine," he answered. "Which means 'like a wolf.'"

"Really?"

"Yeah, really."

I looked down at the lupine. Wolflike. It seemed harmless enough.

My favorite was all over this meadow. There were zillions of orange lilies at the top of stems, their trumpet-shaped flowers held high toward the sky. I really liked the lilies. They made me feel at home, somehow. Maybe because it was the only flower I knew.

We walked through the meadow and kept trekking. We didn't take a break until about mid-morning.

Man, was I glad Mark had made me rub the oil on my back. Everything on my whole body was tired and sore and just about worn out. And we'd only been going for about two hours.

We took our first break beneath a silver fir. There were no big sequoias here. We wouldn't get to those up here, on our way to the pass. Only pines and firs, mostly.

As we sat, I looked up and off into the distance. I could see the side of Sabertooth mountain. There were some scraggly trees jutting out, practically sideways. There wasn't much else growing there.

"What's that?" I asked.

"What?"

"That," I said, pointing off into the distance, toward the mountain.

"You mean Sabertooth?"

"No, the trees."

"Oh, those are dwarf pines. They grow anywhere."

"Anywhere?"

"Just about." Mark nodded. "They can grow upside down, practically. They're the wildest little trees. They'll hang anywhere there's even the tiniest amount of soil and water."

I looked back at the trees with more respect. So. They could grow anywhere?

It was too bad people weren't like that. People were choosy. They had to live where things were just right, where they didn't have to work too hard. Not that dwarf pine, though. It just hung out where it could.

I wanted to be like the dwarf pine. I wanted to be tough enough that I could go anywhere, at any time, and just plant my roots and live. I wanted to be able to hang upside down, practically, on any old mountain slope and make it. That's what I wanted.

Now, it wasn't like I was going to tell anyone about something weird like that. You didn't exactly say things like that out loud. It would sound . . . strange. Especially out here in the middle of the wilderness, with your stepdad.

I looked over at Mark. Did he think about things like that? I wondered. He had to, right? Didn't everybody think about things like that?

We set our packs off to one side. Mark grabbed some jerky and tossed me a piece. I tore into it ravenously.

"Eating with a lupine vengeance, I see," Mark chuckled.

"Huh?"

"Nothin'. Forget it."

I stared at Mark for a second, and then took another bite. It took me another moment before I understood what he'd just said.

"Oh, I get it," I said numbly. "Lupine. Like a wolf."

"There you go."

"Takes me a while sometimes," I muttered.

I looked out over the landscape with satisfaction. I'd made it this far without dropping. My back was sore, and my legs could feel it from the climb. But, overall, I felt fine. No problem. I was starting to get into this.

As we sat there, eating without saying much, a squirrel came toward us. Tentative, hesitating, checking us with every motion, every step, the squirrel inched forward.

The squirrel nosed around in the pine cones that were thick on the ground. Now this animal I knew. I didn't have to ask Mark. It was a Douglas squirrel. It ate all sorts of things—grass seeds, berries, hazelnuts, the seeds of cones.

The squirrel found a large cone, grabbed it, and stood up on its haunches. It held the cone delicately between its two front paws. It rotated the cone forward, like it was eating corn on the cob, and peeled away the scales so it could get at the seeds.

I watched, fascinated. Had the squirrel come to join us? Or was it just in the neighborhood?

I had no idea, really. I would never know. You couldn't about things like that. They just happened.

The Douglas squirrel finished its cone, dropped the depleted, thoroughly explored shell to the ground, and inched forward some more.

When it was within ten feet or so of us, it stopped and just stared at us. Mark and I didn't budge. We stayed rock still and stared back.

Then I had an idea. It occurred to me that I had something in my pack that this squirrel would love. Something it had never tasted before—and never would again, most likely.

I'd brought a huge bag of dry roasted peanuts with me. I knew squirrels loved almost any kind of nut.

They lived for nuts. This squirrel would get a kick out of something dry roasted.

For some reason, I thought about the raccoon back at the house. That dumb old raccoon wouldn't touch these dry roasted peanuts. It always left them untouched.

But I was sure this squirrel would go for them, in a big way. I had no idea why I knew that. It just made sense to me.

Slowly, careful not to make any sudden movements, I reached around and unfastened the Velcro on my pack and slipped the bag of peanuts free. I reached in and palmed one peanut.

The squirrel was eyeing me curiously. It let out a raucous chatter, as if to tell me not to do anything foolish or stupid.

Mark was looking at me, too. I could see him watching me out of the corner of my eye.

I'd learned enough about animals since I'd come to the wild that I knew what it would take to approach this squirrel. One sudden movement, I knew, and it would bolt like lightning.

So I made sure every part of my body that I moved did so in slow motion. When I turned my head, I did it like I was moving slowly under water, or in the slow motion of a video.

I leaned forward and began to crawl toward the squirrel. I stayed low to the ground, so the squirrel could get a good look at me. It still hadn't moved.

I crawled five feet or so, until I was quite close to the squirrel. I didn't stare at it. I would look at it for a moment, look away, and then look back again. I knew that if I stared at it continuously, it would get nervous and take off.

I sat back on my haunches slowly, and then held out the peanut. I held it out in full display, so the squirrel could see exactly what I was offering. Then I dropped it onto a broad leaf that had fallen to the ground. I lifted the leaf up and moved it to a spot halfway between us.

The squirrel gave me one more look and then began to inch toward the leaf. It was genuinely curious. I could see the whiskers on its nose twitching. It could smell that peanut. It *wanted* that peanut.

But could it trust me? That was the question. It was written all over the quivering fur of the squirrel. Every twitch, every movement, spoke volumes about its fear and longing. Boy, did it want that peanut! But at what cost? the squirrel seemed to be asking. Was this some kind of an elaborate trap?

Finally, the sharp aroma of the peanut won out. Plus, it must have figured I was harmless. Because in the end it hopped down onto all fours, scooted over to the leaf, grabbed the peanut, popped it into its mouth, and then scooted away a few feet to savor its newfound delicacy.

I fed three or four more peanuts to the squirrel. With each one, the squirrel got bolder. And closer.

Finally, I held out a peanut in the palm of my hand. The squirrel hesitated for only a moment before it scampered over and took it directly from my hand, its whiskers brushing lightly across my palm, before hurrying back to a safe vantage point.

I decided the squirrel had had enough. I didn't

want to deplete my precious stock of dry roasted peanuts for some dumb squirrel even before we began.

"Shoo, go on," I said softly. The squirrel didn't move. It had grown accustomed to me, and to its feast. So I picked up a pine cone and tossed it. The cone landed about a foot in front of the squirrel, which promptly turned and ran away, chattering a blue streak.

"Well, I never," Mark said.

"Never what?" I asked, turning to face him.

Mark was just staring at me. "I've never seen anything quite like that before, that's for sure."

"Like what?"

"Like you. You're a marvel."

"What're you talkin' about?"

"I've never seen anyone get that close to a wild creature and befriend it so quickly, that's what."

"I was just feedin' it peanuts, like you do at the zoo."

"Yeah, but this isn't the zoo," Mark said in a low voice. "That squirrel's probably only seen a few people in its lifetime, maybe not even that many."

"Aw, you just have to know how to approach it."

"I guess. But I've never seen anyone work it like you just did. It was magic."

I beamed. I'd never really thought about it much. I was only doing what I thought was natural. But it was nice to be complimented. I liked it.

"Anybody could have done it," I said, picking at the dirt.

"I don't think so, Josh," Mark said. "I've never seen it before. You clearly have a way with animals. Like nothing I've ever seen before."

△
CHAPTER 12

△When we left that spot, something had changed. I couldn't tell what it was, exactly. But it was there nevertheless.

It took us most of the afternoon to climb up to King Lakes, which is where we were going to camp for the night. We got there in the late afternoon, with plenty of light and warmth to spare.

I dropped my pack the instant we got to the water's edge. I was bone weary. I was sure I couldn't move another muscle until morning.

"Can't rest now," Mark warned me.

"What?" I asked bleakly.

"Your tent, ace," he laughed.

"Whatcha mean, my tent?"

"Need to put it up now, before you can do anything else."

"Anything else?"

Mark shook his head. "You weren't, like, planning to just lie there for the rest of the day, were you?"

"I was thinkin' about it."

"Well, don't. And we're goin' swimming as soon as you get your tent up."

I looked over at the lake in front of us. It was dead quiet up here. Actually, that wasn't entirely right. There were plenty of sounds. I could hear crickets already, and a couple of frogs. Birds screeched or cawed or cooed every so often. I thought I heard a woodpecker from some part of the forest around the lake.

But there were no city sounds, no car tires squealing or people yelling or doors slamming. Nothing like that.

The lake we'd stopped at wasn't huge. I could see all of it in front of me. The trees practically came down to the edge all the way around. We were on one of the few open sandy parts of the surrounding shoreline.

Mark had said there were a few other smaller lakes just like this one, connected by streams. We would pass by a couple of them in the morning, on the way to Sabertooth Pass.

It seemed hard to imagine that we would find snow in the morning—through the pass—because it was gorgeous and warm here right now.

"We can go swimming here?" I asked.

"Sure, why not?"

I frowned. "I didn't bring my trunks."

"You don't need those."

"What?"

Mark dropped his pack. "Just undershorts."

"Huh?"

"You don't need swimming trunks here." Mark started to break his pack down for the night. He pulled the tent free and tossed it a few feet away. "It's not like anyone's here to see you."

It was weird. I'd never really thought about it. But of course Mark was right. You didn't need fancy trunks here.

Mark put the tent up quickly. He didn't need much help, but I offered it anyway. I pounded in the stakes, and he pulled the ropes taut. We had it up in a jiffy.

Almost the instant we were finished, Mark started to yank his shirt off. "Last one in fixes dinner," he said, his voice muffled from the shirt he was pulling over his head.

"No fair!" I yelled, hurrying to catch him.

Mark didn't answer. He yanked his shirt off and started to work on the rest of his clothes.

I leaped into action. This was my kind of race. I could shuck clothes like crazy. I figured I held the world record for fastest out of school clothes and into play clothes.

I started at the other end. I untied my shoelaces and then kicked both boots off with two quick motions. I pulled both socks off, inside out, with two more. I started to run toward the lake. I pulled my shirt over my head as I ran. I let the shirt fall to the ground.

I'd stomped Mark. He was still struggling to get his own boots off. In one final burst, I made it to the shore. Without hesitating, I leaped high in the air and did a big bellyflop into the water—

"*Aaaggghhh!*" I yelled at the top of my lungs a second later, my voice echoing for miles. Birds scattered. Other creatures cowered in fear, I was sure.

"A little cold?" Mark called out.

"It's *ice* water!" I yelled back. "I'm freezin' my tail off! Why didn't you warn me?"

"You didn't ask."

"You could have told me."

"I suppose I *could* have." Mark smiled broadly as he walked toward the water. Gingerly, he eased his way in. He most certainly didn't run and do a big bellyflop.

I rubbed my arms furiously. I felt like I'd just turned blue all over. I was numb with cold. Goose pimples had broken out all over my body.

I decided I had to get used to the water. I started jumping up and down, submerging and then leaping high in the air. I did it over and over, thrashing my arms as I did so, until I wasn't so cold. It seemed like it took forever.

Mark still hadn't completely gotten in by the time I was finished. So I helped him along. I cupped my hands and sent two waves over the water in his direction.

"Hey!" he yelled.

But I wasn't about to stop. I kept sending waves at him until finally he had no choice, and he too dove beneath the water. He emerged a moment later, shivering and freezing like me. I was thoroughly satisfied.

"By the way, I won," I called to him. "I want a cheeseburger and french fries. And a chocolate milkshake, too."

Mark didn't answer right away. He was too busy slapping his arms against the parts of his body that were freezing.

We must have looked like raving idiots, I figured. But there was no one to see us. So what did it matter? Who would care?

I stopped for a second. I stared at Mark. There was something here, something I *almost* had figured out. I couldn't quite get to it, though.

It had something to do with why you did certain things. Did you do them for other people's benefit? Were you always looking over your shoulder to see if other people approved? Was that it?

Out here, you only had two for an audience—you and God. If you were uncomfortable with either, I figured, then you would struggle a little in a place like this.

So was that it? Did you do things because other people would approve—or, maybe, disapprove? Did you have certain friends, or talk a certain way, or dress a certain way, or act a certain way because other people were watching?

I looked at Mark. He had only his undershorts on, but it didn't seem to matter. I was the only other person here, and he was my stepdad, and I didn't care. It was OK.

And if he yelled at the top of his lungs, well, who would care? The birds and the frogs, maybe.

And what did God think of all this? I felt like, to Him, it made no difference whether you were in the middle of the wilderness or in the middle of a crowded street in Washington, D.C.

I figured He saw you pretty clearly no matter

where you were. The difference was that, out here, I felt like I had a better shot at getting a clear look at Him. Or at least at seeing Him through His creation.

The lake, the birds, the mountain peak off in the distance, the trees lining the lake, the ripples on the water, even the icy chill of the water itself—they all said something to me.

There was perfection here. There was no malice or evil intent in these things, only a goodness that knew no deceit or treachery.

I guess that's why people loved the outdoors. Or why some people did. It was easy to be drawn to it. You could fall in love with this, it was so basic, simple, pure.

But I could *sense* that you had to look beyond, through, around . . . something more. Where there is perfect creation, I knew, there had to be a perfect Creator. There had to be. I was more certain of that at this moment than I ever had been in my life.

In a funny way, I could almost hear God's voice answering back, telling me that I was right. This was His work, His creation. All that I could see, He had created. Down to the very last cricket beginning to chirp happily as the day ended, it belonged to Him.

And He had given it to me. I was now in charge of it. I was its caretaker, its guardian.

I looked around at the landscape. It was an awesome task. How could I possibly be in charge of all of *this*? How? It went on forever, and I was so small, so insignificant. How could I possibly make a difference out here in so vast a place as this?

"Josh, you all right?" Mark asked quietly.

I shook my head sharply and looked over at him. "Oh, yeah, sure."

"You're not too cold?"

"No, no," I said quickly. "I was just thinkin', that's all."

Mark smiled. "It's easy to do out here, isn't it?"

"Yeah, it is."

Mark shook his hair one more time. "I'm headin' in. Time to catch some dinner."

That one got me. "Dinner?"

"You didn't think you were getting off that easy, did you?"

"Um, I guess not. So what's for dinner?"

"Whatever you catch."

"But you said the loser had to fix dinner." I groaned.

"*Fix* dinner," laughed Mark. "I didn't say anything about *catching* it."

△ CHAPTER 13

△While Mark rigged the fishing pole he'd brought with him, I scrabbled for worms under big rocks. I figured it would take me forever to catch something. I was lousy at fishing.

But I was wrong. They bit like crazy in this little lake. Maybe it was because they hadn't seen too many fishermen. I didn't know.

But within five minutes after I'd cast my line from some weeds near the shore, I had my first bluegill. It was *huge*. I'd caught bluegills before, but they'd never been so large. A half an hour later, I had three more. And we had our dinner.

I let Mark kill and clean them. I felt a little squeamish. Mark didn't even hesitate. He clubbed the fish once to knock them senseless. Then he took his long knife and, with one clean swipe, cut off their heads.

Next, he slit open their bellies and pulled the guts

111

free. He tossed them out into the water. Using the sharp blade of the knife, he scraped off the scales. Then he handed the remaining slabs of meat to me.

"What do I do with these?" I asked.

"Go wash 'em, of course."

I did as he said. The chunks of flesh I held in my hand didn't much seem like the quivering fish I'd so recently caught. They almost seemed like two totally different things.

Mark had a fire going by the time I got back. He'd brought some tin foil with him, and he partially wrapped the fish up and then set them in the coals of the fire.

"They'll cook that way?" I asked.

"Sure, why not? As good as any other way."

"Whatcha puttin' in them?"

"A few rocks and pebbles, maybe a little dirt and sand mixed in?"

"I'm serious."

"So am I."

I scuffed at the dirt. "You really didn't bring anything else?"

Mark looked around. He spotted something. "I can't help you with the fish. You'll have to eat it as it is. You'll like it. Trust me. Your appetite is different here. But we can spice up the atmosphere a little. There's some mountain mint over there."

"Mountain mint?"

Mark pointed over to a spot about fifty feet away. There were clusters of white or purple flowers throughout the weeds and tall grass. "Those?" I asked.

"Those."

I walked over to the clusters. I reached down and plucked a handful. The sweet smell of mint practically jumped into the air.

"Hey, cool," I yelled to Mark.

"You can set the table with them," he called back.

I walked over to the fire. "The table?"

Mark gestured at the ground. "Sure. Set 'em up on our table."

I piled the flowers up on the ground, about ten feet from the fire. Then I stood by the fire and watched the fish cook. Mark had peeled the tin foil back a little. It was interesting to watch the fish roast.

Mark turned the fish once, to keep them from burning. He just reached in with his fingers and flipped them. I was surprised that he didn't burn his fingers.

"You seem to know what you're doin' out here," I said as Mark set the fish down at our "table."

Mark gave me a curious look. "What did you think I was doing all those years before I met your mother?"

I was staring at my fish. I wasn't exactly sure what I was supposed to do now. I had no knife and fork, no salt and pepper. "I dunno," I mumbled.

"I spent most of my time doing just this," Mark said. "I went out every chance I had."

"By yourself?"

"Sure. Why not?"

"You weren't worried?"

"About what?"

I shrugged. "Beats me. It just seems like you could get lonely."

Mark looked around again. The light was starting

113

to fade, but that just brought the colors out all the more. Purple, yellow, orange, maroon—there was color everywhere, in any direction you chose to look.

"How could you be lonely out here?" Mark said softly. "There is life everywhere. More here than anywhere on earth. It spills out over every single edge and precipice."

"I guess."

"No, you know it, Josh. Especially you. I can see it in you, kid. You appreciate a place like this as much as anyone I've ever run across."

I could feel my collar getting hot. I was sure my face was turning red. Part of me knew Mark was right. I did feel right at home out here. This was my place. But it was hard for me to admit.

"You think there's any snow in the pass?" I asked, changing the subject.

"They tell me the snow isn't blocking the pass," Mark said.

I'd watched him eat his fish. He hadn't even hesitated. He'd just grabbed one of the filets with both hands and taken a big bite.

I reached down gingerly and picked up my own piece. I held it up to my mouth, plugged my nose, and took a bite. It practically melted in my mouth.

"Hey, this is good," I said, somewhat surprised. The fish wasn't tough or stringy, like some you got at the supermarket. It practically broke up in your mouth as you ate it.

"What did you expect?" Mark laughed.

"I dunno. Not this."

I devoured the fish. I finished well ahead of Mark. I

was ready for more. But of course this was all I'd caught.

Mark saw the look on my face. "Don't worry, Josh. I'm not completely heartless. I did bring a few things you might be interested in."

"Yeah, like what?"

Mark hopped up and went over to his backpack. He grabbed something from the backpack and tossed it through the air toward me. I could tell what it was, from the red and white wrapper, even as it hurtled through the air toward me.

It was a Baby Ruth bar, my favorite. "All right!" I yelled. "Man, this is great."

Mark just smiled as I tore off the wrapper. The fish was great. No question about it. But I was glad we hadn't totally forgotten about the world we'd come from, either.

△
CHAPTER 14

△We'd stayed up another hour as it got dark, just lying on our backs, staring at the stars. It was nice lying there, side by side, close to the fire, not saying anything.

It was strange to discover that I didn't have to talk to Mark. I would never have guessed that we could get along like that. It was easy with Ashley. We thought alike. But Mark? I wouldn't have figured it.

I mean, he was my *stepdad*. How could he be my friend, too?

We set off first thing in the morning, when the dew was still heavy in the tall grass and there was a chill in the air and frost on the rocks. The sun had not yet made its way over the top of the mountains in the distance.

I hated getting out of my sleeping bag to get

dressed. It was cold even inside the tent. I couldn't even imagine what it was like outside.

In the end, it was the smell of the toasting bagels and coffee that had gotten me up and out. I'd hurried into my blue jeans and sweatshirt as fast as I could. I'd figured I could change into hiking shorts later, when it was warmer.

Mark let me have half a cup of coffee with my bagels. He made me promise not to tell Mom. I poured in lots of the sugar Mark had brought along just for his coffee, and sipped it carefully. It was nasty stuff. I wasn't exactly sure why people drank it. There had to be something about it that I didn't understand.

The night's sleep had done wonders for me. The pack felt lighter, my step was faster. I felt better all around.

It took us nearly four hours—straight uphill—to get to the pass. We passed two more lakes after we'd left our camping site. The path was even harder to follow up here, but Mark seemed to have no problem. He had a sixth sense about where to go.

I just stared up as we walked along toward the jagged rocks that marked Sabertooth Peak. You could see them quite clearly now. The pass went practically right through the peak.

We reached the pass just before noon. It was partially filled with snow, but I could see that you could still walk through. It had melted enough to get by.

I couldn't believe that it was July, and that there was still snow here. It was unbelievable to me. But there was hard-packed snow clearly visible all over the peak, and it extended well down into the pass.

In fact, there was quite a lot of it hanging over the pass. There was one part, especially, where the sides of the pass seemed to go straight up toward the peak. And on that part, there seemed to be plenty of snow.

"Is it safe?" I asked Mark just as we entered the pass.

Mark didn't say anything right away. He could see the same part of the pass I could, where the sides were quite steep and where there was still a lot of snow packed to them.

"We'll need to keep a lookout," he said somberly.

I didn't like that answer. "For what?"

"For any kind of movement. If you see *anything*, you let me know. OK?"

"Yeah, sure, OK. But what am I lookin' for, exactly?"

Mark pointed to the part of the pass where the snow was the thickest, at the steep incline about halfway through the pass. "If you see snow moving over the top, or maybe a few big rocks sliding across the top, you let me know."

"What will it mean? If I see something like that?"

Mark didn't say anything for a moment. He was still studying the landscape intensely. I could see he was definitely concerned, though he was trying not to let it show.

"When snow is melting like this," Mark said slowly, "sometimes there's movement up higher, where the snow stays year-round."

"Movement? Like an avalanche or something?"

Mark nodded. "Yes, an avalanche. It usually takes something to set one off. Have you ever been snow skiing in a place where they use big guns to set off avalanches?"

I shook my head. I'd never been snow skiing, period, much less in a place where they used guns to start avalanches.

"Well," Mark continued, "what they do is fire these blasts into the side of a mountain, and let the snow slide."

I looked back up at the part of the pass where there was a lot of snow. "And that's what it would take here, something like that?"

"I don't know," mused Mark. "I just don't know. We should be able to just walk right through. But I still want you to keep a lookout. OK?"

"OK. But can we eat some lunch first?"

Mark hesitated. I could see he was anxious to get through the pass. But he was hungry, too. "All right," he said. He slipped his pack off and plopped it on the ground. "We'll eat first."

"Great." I let my pack slide to the ground, too.

Mark surprised me one more time. He'd packed huge peanut butter and jelly sandwiches, for both of us. And he had apples, too. I wondered how much more food he was carrying in there that I didn't know about.

We both ate in grateful silence. The walk to the pass had been hard, and I was pretty worn out. It was nice to know that we'd mostly be working our way down the other side of the mountain once we were through the pass.

After I finished my lunch, I stood up to stretch. I walked over to the side, where heavy grass skirted the trail.

120

I wasn't doing anything in particular. I was just wandering. It was nice to walk around without a pack strapped to my back.

I looked down at the ground. My heart practically stopped beating. My breath got short. I couldn't believe I hadn't seen this before.

There were tracks everywhere, lots of them. They were all in single file, but I could see that there were probably about six or seven of them, running hard.

Wolves. I was sure of the track. The footpad was like a triangle, with the points rounded. Then there were four toes, with a claw at the end of each.

But there hadn't been any wolves in these parts for years. I knew that. There were some gray wolves in Arizona, but not in these parts. No wolves had been this far west or south for a long, long time. So what was this?

"Hey, Mark," I called softly. "Come check this out."

Mark sauntered over. He too stopped cold when he saw the tracks. "Well, I'll be," he said.

"What?"

"I'd heard about these, but I wouldn't have believed it if I hadn't seen them for myself."

"They're wolves, right?" I asked.

Mark just whistled. "No, not really. They're half-breeds. Part wolf, part coyote."

"I've never heard of such a thing," I said, incredulous.

"It's true. It's been happening some over the past ten years or so. The wolves down in Mexico or out in Arizona breed with some of the coyotes. Then you get a critter like this."

121

"How can you tell?"

Mark knelt down on the ground. He pointed at one of the tracks. "First, see the size. It's definitely bigger than a coyote. Plus, the toes and claws are further away from the footpad than they would be if it was a coyote."

"So how do you know this isn't a wolf?" I asked.

"You don't, really. Except we haven't had any wolves around here practically forever. At least that's what the other rangers tell me."

I looked back down at the track. It sure looked like a wolf track. But maybe Mark was right.

"So if it's a half-breed, how will it act?"

Mark shrugged. "Who knows? But if it's traveling in a pack, I'd guess more like a wolf."

"Coyotes run in packs, too," I offered.

"Occasionally. But not very often, especially in summer like this."

I stood up. I eyeballed the length between the tracks. It looked considerable. "Think they were runnin' hard?"

Mark measured the distance as I had. He nodded. "Looks that way."

"So what were they running from?"

Mark looked around. The place was as silent right now as it ever got, with just an occasional bird call. "Most likely, they were running *to* something."

"But what?"

Mark looked over at me. "Perhaps we'll find out."

"I hope not." I shivered at the thought. Whether they were wolves or coyotes, or something in between, it wouldn't be fun to meet up with a pack out here. Not fun at all.

I knew we were both thinking the same thing as we walked back to our packs. If we ran into a wolf pack—or whatever these creatures were—we'd be in a heap of trouble. Especially if they were hunting or angry.

I hadn't asked, but I was pretty sure Mark didn't have a gun with him. He didn't carry one with him when he went camping, even out here in the deeper parts of the wilderness.

All he had with him was a fairly wicked hunting knife. It was a great knife—sharp and long, with a sturdy shaft. But it would be no match for a pack of half-breed wolves. There wasn't much you could do if they all came at you.

My mind started to race with possibilities. I knew they weren't likely to come at us, especially during the day. At night, we could switch off keeping a fire tended.

That would be awful, having to alternate sleeping to make sure the fire didn't die. But if we had to, I was prepared.

And if they came at us during the day, what then? I had no idea. I guess we'd have to cross that bridge when we got there.

"Let's go," Mark said quietly once he'd secured his pack.

I noticed, out of the corner of my eye, that Mark had quickly reached into his pack and secured his knife. He tried to pull it out so that I couldn't see. But I noticed anyway. Mark had left it in its sheath, but he'd attached it to his belt loop so that he could get to it quickly.

I didn't say anything to him about it. I just hoped we wouldn't need it.

Before we set off, I scoured the ground for the heaviest stick I could find. I spied a fresh limb and broke off one end. It proved to be a pretty sturdy club about two feet long, with a knob at the end. It was better than nothing, I figured.

Mark looked over at me. He nodded once, approving. "Good idea," he said tightly.

"Just in case," I answered.

"Let's hope you don't have to use it."

△
CHAPTER 15

△As we walked, I watched Mark like a hawk. I was surprised to see the change that had come over him. He was practically a different person. He was all business. I could see he was paying close attention to everything he saw.

His face was a grim mask of concentration. His eyes were narrowed, focused on the path through the pass. His walk was careful and deliberate. He was looking for signs everywhere, anything that said the pack might be close by.

It was startling to behold. I thought I knew Mark. But I'd never seen this fierce warrior before.

Because that was what he looked like. He was ready to defend his life—or perhaps to defend mine. I could see that every part of him was engaged. He was totally alive.

I was too, but I was also scared. I had no idea what

to expect. Perhaps nothing. Perhaps something I couldn't possibly grasp.

I'd read about wolf packs. They could track prey for days. They would wait patiently, if they had to.

But they almost never hunted man. They knew instinctively that it meant death to their pack when they did. So they tended to avoid man whenever possible.

But that wasn't always the case. There had been times when a pack would turn on humans, especially out in a remote area like this. It did happen. It would take something extraordinary to set them off, I knew, but it wasn't like it was out of the question.

"You set?" Mark asked me.

I nodded and shifted the backpack one last time. We both started walking into the pass.

"Let me go first," Mark said. "OK?"

"Got it."

Mark moved in front of me. I glanced at his hands. He was rubbing his thumb across his fingertips as he walked. I'd never seen him do that.

Mark had said it would take us close to forty-five minutes to make it all the way through the pass, and about twenty minutes or so to get past the point where much of the snow was still hanging.

Every so often, I checked the edge of the path, to make sure the pack had still come this way. I kept hoping that maybe the tracks weren't as fresh as they looked, and that maybe the pack had doubled back for some reason and were no longer out in front of us.

But every time I checked, the tracks were still there. And they looked even fresher through here, with flecks of dirt newly kicked up around some of the marks where claws had dug into the ground.

As we neared the halfway point through the pass, Mark's pace quickened just a little. I could see he was anxious to get through here, though I wasn't sure why.

There was an outcropping of rock just in front of us, and the path turned fairly hard left after it. Mark stopped for a moment, pointed to it, and said softly, "It's downhill after that turn."

"Great," I answered.

I glanced at the spot again before we set off. From the outcropping, the mountain face was sheer. It went straight up, to a spot where the snow was heaviest. On the right, though, it was a gradual, 45-degree incline over rock shards. There were a couple of dwarf pines clinging to the soil in that direction.

Just before we turned the corner, Mark stiffened. He'd heard something. An uneasy chill swept through me. Though I hadn't heard anything, I trusted Mark's instincts completely. I stopped by his side and waited.

"Do you hear it?" he whispered to me.

I listened intently. Finally, after about a minute, I heard it too.

It was both a clicking and a scraping sound. *Click*, then scrape. *Click*, then scrape. It seemed totally out of place here.

I knew of no animal that made a sound like that. It definitely wasn't a bird. But what could it be?

"A squirrel, maybe, trying to break a nut on a rock?" I said.

Mark shook his head. His eyes had a faraway glaze

to them, like he was listening for some answer with both his eyes and his mind at the same time. "No, there's something else, besides the scraping."

I listened again. Mark was right. I heard it finally. It was a tearing sound. Like the sound a dog makes when it is trying to keep you from pulling a tennis ball from its mouth.

I closed my eyes for a moment. Every nerve in my body was screaming. I wanted to just turn and run back down the path as fast as I could. I wanted to get away from this spot, and never return.

"Don't move," Mark ordered quietly through clenched teeth. "And don't run. That would definitely set them off."

I tried to swallow. I couldn't. My mouth was so dry my tongue stuck to my teeth. My breath was coming in shallow gasps.

Mark pulled the knife free of its sheath. I held onto my little club with both hands, prepared for the worst.

We edged around the corner. I was right at Mark's side. Less than a foot separated us. Mark peered around the corner. I did too, a moment later.

Fifty feet on the other side, to the left of the pass, was the pack of half-breed wolves. They were all gathered around something. There were six or seven of them, slightly bigger than coyotes, but definitely not full-sized wolves.

They were pulling and tearing at something, in unison. But it didn't look like a deer or an animal they'd tracked and killed. No, it was something else.

Mark and I stared for the longest time, trying to

128

figure out what was happening as they systematically ripped at whatever it was.

Two of the half-breeds paused for a second, giving me a good glimpse of the object of their attention. At that moment, I understood. And I realized that we were probably in trouble.

I pulled back behind the rock outcropping. Mark did too. He'd seen it as well.

"One of them's in a trap," I whispered. "Did you see it?"

Mark nodded. "I did. And they're trying to free it. But they'll never get it free. Never."

"Why?"

"Did you see what kind of trap it was?"

"No, what?"

"It was one of those old bear traps, with the big thirty- or forty-pound bars that crush the animal. That's what has one of them pinned. There's no way they'll get it free. And even if they do, its legs have to be crushed."

"So what do we do now?"

I was scared. There was no way around it. Mark looked at me. He saw it in my eyes. "We'll get past this. It'll be all right. Just trust me. Follow my lead. OK?"

I nodded. I did trust Mark. I would do exactly as he said. No matter what happened next.

"Now," Mark continued, "here's what we're gonna do. When they spot us—and they will, eventually, I want you to run up to one of those dwarf pines on the other side of the pass. Just scramble on up to it, and hold on. It'll make it harder for them to charge at you. OK?"

"Got it."

"Then, once they're away from the trap and down below you, I'll take a run at the trap from the other tree. I think I can lift the bar free. Maybe that will distract the pack long enough for us to get free and clear."

"Will it work?" I asked, trying not to let my panic edge into my voice.

"It'll have to," Mark said.

"And if it doesn't?"

Mark looked at me directly. He wanted to make sure I understood. "Then we fight them. Josh, they kill by going for the throat. Don't let 'em near your throat. And don't run. Not for any reason. They can run twice as fast as you, and they'll drag you down from behind."

"I understand. I won't run."

"Keep your club in front of you. Don't swing it at them unless you have to. Let me use my knife to attack. OK?"

"OK."

Mark smiled. It wasn't much of a smile, but at least it was a smile. "Hey, look. I think there's a pretty good chance that they'll make a bluff charge, and then take off. They won't want to pick a fight with us, or this knife. We have to just make sure we don't back down from the start. So are you ready?"

"Yeah, let's do it."

We edged around the corner. I glanced to my right and measured the distance. It wasn't far, maybe fifteen feet, to the edge of the pass and then maybe five steps up the slope to the dwarf pine.

The pack was scrabbling hard to free one of its own

from the trap. They still weren't paying attention to us.

They were all about three feet or so long, with reddish gray fur, and rusty legs, ears, and feet. Their throats and bellies were whitish. Their noses weren't quite as pointed as a coyote's would be, and their ears were slightly smaller.

After a few minutes, almost on cue, they all seemed to just take a break. They backed off from the trap, sat down on their haunches, and let their tongues hang as they caught their breath.

One of them glanced over in our direction. It sprang to its feet immediately. It held its head high, its neck arched. Its shoulder and neck hairs stood straight up, like a bristle brush. It let out a guttural *yip* followed by a deep growl.

The others quickly spotted us as well. They closed ranks almost instantly, and began to gather for a charge. They weren't waiting, maybe because they were so angry over what had happened to one of the members of their pack.

"Go up the slope. Now!" Mark commanded.

I moved to my right immediately. The half-breed wolves took two tentative steps, and then charged. I ran for the slope. I took five or six hard steps up it, grabbed hold of the pine, and then swung around to face them.

Mark hadn't run. He'd taken the charge. He slashed out with his knife once, catching one of them on the back. He slashed again, nipping a second. The pack backed off instantly, surrounding him. They crouched, their bellies low to the ground, and growled.

131

Mark eased his way to the slope as well, never turning away from the pack. He walked up the slope backward until he'd reached the second dwarf pine.

The pack wasn't sure what to do now. They clearly didn't want to leave their fallen pack member, and they also didn't want to face that knife again. I could see from where I stood that Mark had gotten the first half-breed with the knife slash. There was blood pouring from a wound. One of the others was licking at it even as we waited.

The pack looked at Mark, then at me and back to Mark. They settled on me. I was smaller, and I didn't have a knife in my hand.

"Back to the tree!" Mark yelled at me as he saw the animals begin to shift their attention in my direction.

I shifted the backpack so that it was plastered up against the tree, and so I was facing downhill. I held the club out in front of me, as Mark had told me to do.

Two of the half-breeds made an initial charge at me up the slope. It wasn't easy for them. Their claws skidded on the rock. I could see that they wouldn't be able to get a foothold and come at me. I swung the club at them as they got near. It grazed one of them, knocking it off-stride. The other turned and half-stumbled, half-skidded back down the slope.

Three more made a charge at me. I swung the club twice more, knocking it into one. One half-breed reached for the club and almost yanked it free of my hand. I only clung to it at the last moment.

All of them then gathered at the foot of the slope, completely ignoring me for the moment. Mark made his move, because there obviously wasn't any time to waste.

He ran straight for the trap. Without even hesitating, he reached down, grabbed a leather strap at the end of the bar that had crushed the legs of the half-breed wolf and pulled as hard as he could. The leather strap snapped, coming free in his hand, but not before the heavy bar rolled free, thudding to the ground on the other side of the fallen half-breed wolf. The animal didn't move. It was probably dead already.

The pack turned as one, just as the bar hit the ground. With yips and yelps filling the air, they turned and made straight for Mark. He took three steps backward and took the charge with his knife in front. He slashed out, catching the nose of the first animal that got to him.

The others stopped immediately. Two of them went over and sniffed at the poor creature that had been caught in the trap.

Mark got distracted for a moment when two of them made a second charge. He turned a little to his right to take the new charge. Just at that moment, one of them slipped behind Mark from the other direction. It started to move toward Mark's back.

Every nerve in my body went crazy. It was like I was on fire. I didn't know what else to do. I couldn't just wait on the slope, cowering under this tree, while the pack went after Mark.

A sound like none I'd ever made came hurtling from my lungs and my mouth. It was like the call of some wild creature. *"Aaarrrggghhh!"* I yelled. The sound rang from treetop to treetop, scaring the birds, scaring the pack. Scaring me.

I sprinted down the slope and ran, pell-mell, straight into the pack. I got to the half-breed behind Mark just before it could leap onto his back. I let out a second horrible yell and swung my club at it. There was a solid *crack* as my club connected with its skull.

The force of the swing knocked me and the half-breed over. We both fell. Before the others could close in on me, though, Mark stepped in front and brandished his knife. None of the pack took the charge.

There was a deep *crack* and a groaning sound above us. It was like the earth had moved. In fact, there was a brief shudder beneath our feet, and the cracking and groaning seemed to go on forever.

The pack started to whine. This was something totally new, different from anything they'd ever heard. They began to edge away from us, back toward the other direction of the pass, where Mark and I had come from. The part-wolf, part-coyote creature that had been caught in the trap still had not moved.

There was a huge *crash!* directly above us, and then a second one. That was enough for the pack. They turned on their heels and sprinted back down the path, away from us.

Mark glanced up once. I did too. We both saw it coming. My yell had set an avalanche in motion. The rocks were starting to tumble down the slope, and bits of snow and rock shards were already starting to rain on us.

"Run, Josh, run!" Mark yelled at me.

I didn't need to be told twice. I began to run as fast

as I could down the path, in the opposite direction from the pack. Mark was close on my heels. He grabbed my hand and propelled me faster, propping me up so I wouldn't trip.

We'd gotten maybe two or three hundred feet down the path when the avalanche hit. It came crashing down with the mightiest roar I'd ever heard. It smashed and tumbled and *whomped* as it came down.

But we were free and clear of it by then. The avalanche was only at that point in the pass, in the narrowest part. It didn't fall anywhere else, really.

We stopped in the sudden silence and turned around to see what had happened. Flakes of snow and powder drifted far up into the sky and all around us.

Snow filled the pass, maybe thirty feet high. There was no way the pack would get past that. No way at all. We'd made it.

CHAPTER 16

It was time to find the Surelock hunters. I knew it. Ashley knew it. I didn't care if anyone else knew it.

The strap that had come loose in Mark's hand, just before the avalanche hit, had lettering stitched into its worn, faded leather. "Surelock," it had said. The "r" and the "o" were all but gone, though, from heavy use or age, or both.

Mark said it was an old, old bear trap, the kind that hadn't been used in forty or fifty years. He'd seen a bear trap like it once, tacked up to someone's old barn. But he couldn't remember where he'd seen it, or whose barn he'd seen it on.

I'd thought about it for the rest of the trip, past huge, magnificent Columbia Lake, around the rim of Ghost Canyon and back down the High Sierra trail.

The half-breed pack of wolves hadn't been able to find us again.

Mark said that once their path through the pass was blocked, they'd have to travel twenty miles to get through another one. That was fine by me.

As Mark thought about what had happened in the pass, he was convinced that someone had laid that old bear trap to catch some big animal deep in the wilderness. Like a bear, maybe. You had to go deep to get a big animal like that, Mark said.

Almost from the minute I got back, Ashley and I began mapping out a plan for how we'd find the Surelock hunters.

The raccoon was up and moving around in our garage now, thanks to Mom's feeding. Pretty soon, it would be well enough to return to the wilderness. Mom said we had to turn it loose as soon as possible, before it got too used to home cooking.

"We've gotta find them," Ashley just kept muttering the night I got back, as we were wandering around on the mountain behind our houses.

"Yeah, I know." I nodded. "But how?"

"You know, we oughta just get on our bikes and go around until we find somebody who's ever had a bear trap."

I groaned. "Man, that could take forever."

"You got a better idea?"

I thought for a moment. And then it occurred to me. I don't know why I hadn't thought about it before.

"Yeah, I do," I said eagerly. "The Checkers Gang'll know."

* * *

138

They were there, like always. The four of them, sitting at the end of the porch at the General Store. They were playing rummy today.

"Howdy," Willis greeted us with a big smile.

"Mornin'," Graddy said.

Doc and Sid looked up from their game, nodded once, and then looked back down. I almost laughed. These were serious card players.

Rachel and the boys weren't out in front of the General Store this time. That suited me just fine. I wasn't comfortable around them to begin with. I didn't particularly feel like another confrontation.

"What's on your minds, kids?" Graddy asked. Both he and his constant playing partner, Willis, leaned back in their chairs and paused in their card game. Doc and Sid kept playing, of course.

"We have a question," Ashley said quickly.

"A question?" Graddy asked.

"Actually, a story," I offered. I quickly recounted the story of the half-breed wolf pack and the bear trap. Graddy and Willis listened silently.

"An old bear trap, you say?" Willis asked when I was finished.

I nodded. "Yeah, and my stepdad said it's the kind you'd see tacked up on the back of an old barn or somethin'."

Willis looked over at their counterparts at the other table. "Sid, remember the Surelock traps we were talking about the other day?" Sid nodded, without looking up. "You ever remember seeing a big one, a Surelock bear trap maybe, up on someone's barn?"

"Yep," Sid answered. "Sure do."

"Well, *where* did you see one?" Willis asked impatiently.

"The old Keenan place," Sid said. "Sam Keenan. He had one on his barn, if I recall."

Ashley and I exchanged glances. Mr. Wilson had told us about the Keenan place. He'd had a bear trap on the back of his barn. Could it be a Surelock?

I looked over at Willis. "Is Sam Keenan's place far from here?"

Willis shook his head. "Nope, a couple of miles from here at best. Take Main Street west from here, look for an old shed, then turn down a dirt road and go another mile or so. It's just on the other side of the railroad tracks that run through there."

I looked back at Willis. "Why didn't he tell us about this place before, when we were here?" I asked quietly.

"Hey, Sid!" Willis called out. "Why didn't you tell 'em about the old Keenan place the last time they were here?"

Sid didn't look up. "They didn't ask."

There weren't many houses west of Jupiter. We found the old shed easily enough, though. There wasn't anything else near it two miles west of the town.

We turned our bikes down the dirt road and headed toward the Keenan farm. The dirt road was muddy and rutted. There was trash all along the side of the road, lots of it. It was disgusting. Why would people just dump stuff out of their car like that?

We'd gone about half a mile when we saw them.

140

Ashley saw them first and came to a skidding stop. I stopped an instant later.

But it was too late. They'd seen us. We couldn't just turn around and head back.

"Ash-heap!" Rachel called out derisively. "Whatcha doin' around here?"

Rachel and the two older boys we'd seen, Dunk and Shawn, were sitting on a rickety old bridge over a muddy creek. Their legs were dangling over the sides, their feet not quite touching the water. Rachel was still wearing no shoes, and the others were letting their gym shoes get soaked by the water. They didn't seem to care.

I admit it. I was afraid. Especially of Dunk, who was easily a foot taller than me. Even more than that, I was afraid of what was sitting next to them—a mangy German shepherd with matted gray and brown hair. The dog was sitting next to Rachel. But it was eyeing us warily.

Even though we were about fifty feet away, Rachel saw me glance at the German shepherd. A wicked grin spread across her face.

"You ain't scared of old Prince here, are you?" she called out. Neither of us answered. I didn't even glance over at Ashley. I could sense her fear.

Rachel reached down and gave the German shepherd a light tap on the top of its head. The dog jerked a little, like it had been shocked. Then she looked up. "Sic 'em!" she yelled gleefully.

The dog leaped to its feet, every hair bristling. It snarled and started to run toward us. Ashley screamed at the top of her lungs and began frantically trying to find the pedals so that she could get away.

The strangest calm came over me. I didn't try to find my own bike pedals. In fact, I didn't even think about trying to get away.

Instead, I stepped from my bike and moved directly in front of Ashley. I stood tall, facing the dog still rushing at us. I had no idea what I meant to do. But, for the strangest reason, I felt no fear. Only a sense of what I had to do.

When the dog closed to within fifteen feet or so, I clapped my hands and yelled in the loudest, most authoritative voice I could muster, "Go away!"

Miraculously, the dog came skidding to a stop. I stood there, watching the dog cautiously. It sat down on its haunches, staring at us. But it was no longer set to charge us. It had heeded my voice.

"Get 'em, boy!" Rachel called out angrily. "You stupid dog, don't just stop!"

"The dog ain't stupid," Shawn growled.

"Well, why'd it stop, then?" Rachel whined.

Dunk stood up. He just glared at the two of them. "Prince! Come here, boy!" The dog turned at the sound of Dunk's voice. It stood up and trotted back to its master.

I didn't move. Ashley was still poised to flee. But I wasn't about to turn and run. I wanted to see the old Keenan place, now more than ever. "Let's go," I said, climbing back onto my bike. "Let's go see the Keenan place."

"But they'll never let us past," Ashley said, her voice still trembling.

"It's a free country," I said. "They can't stop us."

I started to pedal my bike toward the bridge. Ashley followed silently behind me.

Rachel and Dunk were arguing as we got to them. Rachel was mad that Dunk had called the dog back.

"Prince is *my* dog, not yours," Dunk said angrily. "So shut your trap, and don't go orderin' my dog around."

"Yeah, but we're feedin' the thing with my money," I heard Rachel say.

"It ain't all yours," Dunk warned ominously. "I got the—"

Rachel stopped and looked up as we approached. "Where do ya think you're headed? This is a private road."

"No, it isn't," I said firmly. I kept pedaling. I wasn't about to stop now.

Dunk stepped in front of our paths. "You can't go this way."

I still didn't stop. I was so close to them now that I could smell them. They reeked of all sorts of things, smells I couldn't even place. Weird, wild, outdoor smells.

Dunk reached out a hand. I brushed past it. He tried to grab a fistful of my shirt. I shook loose and kept pedaling. I thought for a moment Dunk was going to come after me, but he decided not to in the end. Ashley breezed past a moment later.

"You won't make it past us so easily on the way back," Dunk warned. "We'll be waitin' for ya."

"You're dead now," Rachel laughed. "Dunk don't take no prisoners."

Somehow, I believed her. But we'd cross that bridge when we got there, I figured. Right now, we had to go visit the old Keenan place.

CHAPTER 17

△Thankfully, Mr. Keenan was there. It would have been awful if we'd come all this way and he'd been gone.

In fact, both Mr. and Mrs. Keenan were there, out back, hanging out wash to dry. There were shirts and pants and all sorts of things flying in the breeze.

The Keenans looked to be in their seventies. He was balding, with just a little bit of white hair left. He was in overalls. She had steel-gray hair. She wore a plaid cotton dress that hung down below her knees. Simple, plain folk.

"Mr. Keenan?" I called out. I let my bike fall to the ground and began to walk toward the two of them. Ashley was right behind.

"That's me, son," he answered, looking up from his task for the moment. "We don't get many visitors around here. What brings you by?"

I got right to it. "Sid said you might know something about an old Surelock bear trap."

"Sid? From the General Store?" I nodded. A big smile lit across Mr. Keenan's face. "Well, tell ole Sid hello for me next time you're in town. Haven't seen him in a while."

"I will," I promised. "So do you know anything about an old bear trap?"

Mr. Keenan stopped and walked over toward us. He looked at both of us for the longest time without saying anything. "The two of you know what kinda trouble you're gettin' into?"

"What do you mean?" I asked. "What trouble?"

Mr. Keenan looked at us again. I liked his eyes. They were gentle and kind, though a bit worn around the edges. But it was what was inside that counted.

"Follow me," he said softly. "I have something to show you."

He turned and began walking toward an old barn that stood at the edge of their place. The barn was huge, but falling apart. It had obviously been run-down for some time.

Mr. Keenan walked slowly to the other side of the barn, away from the house and the road. We followed behind silently. I had no idea what was going on here.

When we got to the other side, we stopped. Mr. Keenan looked out into the woods, then back to the barn. He looked up at a spot on the wall. Ashley and I looked as well.

There was nothing on the wall. Nothing, except for an old faded outline of something that had obviously been hanging there for a very long time.

"I kept the Surelock hanging here," Mr. Keenan said slowly. "Been there since we moved here twenty years ago."

"Twenty years?" I said softly.

"Twenty years, and nary a problem," he answered. "Never locked my doors once, never even thought about it."

We all looked back at the empty spot on the wall. The Surelock was obviously gone now.

"How long's it been gone?" Ashley asked.

Mr. Keenan sighed. "Oh, I guess a couple of months. Somethin' like that."

"Did you tell the sheriff?" Ashley asked.

Mr. Keenan started laughing. "What? That a worthless old trap was stolen? It ain't worth a dime. They'd just laugh me out of town. No, I thought about it, 'specially after the other traps were stolen a few days later. But I didn't."

Ashley and I both looked at each other sharply. "The other traps?" she and I asked practically at the same time.

Mr. Keenan waved us on. We followed him as he trooped through the tall grass until he'd gotten to a side door. He ducked inside. The air was musty in the barn.

"I kept 'em all over there, in that corner," he said, pointing to a spot in the corner of the barn. There was nothing there.

"Traps?" I asked.

"Yep, 'bout thirty or forty of 'em," Mr. Keenan said. "Bought 'em all when the company went outta business. Don't think anyone around here 'cept me has hung onto the Surelocks. Never used 'em, though. Not much good with 'em, I guess."

"And someone stole them?" I said, asking the obvious question.

Mr. Keenan nodded. "But I couldn't begin to tell ya why they'd want 'em. Old and rusted, they were. Not much use to anyone."

Ashley and I looked at each other. I felt sure we were both thinking the same thing. The question, though, was how we'd prove it. And what we'd do *then*.

△
CHAPTER 18

△We'd managed to make it away from the Keenan farm by biking through the woods, away from the bridge. It had given us a chance to look at the land surrounding the farm anyway.

It hadn't been difficult getting away. We'd worked our way to a creek. Then, using the compass that I now carried with me religiously whenever I was out, we worked our way north and east until we'd come to the outskirts of town. Rachel and Dunk would have to wait.

It was weird. It was all beginning to make sense now. Like this huge jigsaw puzzle you've been working on forever. None of the pieces seem to fit, and then—*wham!*—all of a sudden, they start falling in place.

As Ashley and I started talking, comparing notes about what we'd seen, the pieces fell.

First, there was the fact that Rachel's great-grandfather had been living in the woods for so long. That would explain how they knew the ways of the forest so well.

Then there was something about their grandfather being laid off from the railroad. That would explain the old railroad spike.

Then there was what that kid had said about letting Dunk and Shawn rip up his old guitar, and the guitar string we'd found with the first snare trap.

Plus, there were the tracks—the gym shoes around the badger trap and then the bare, human feet and the gym shoes around the raccoon trap behind our homes.

Then there was Rachel talking about the money they'd made, doing something. And, finally, there were the stolen traps.

It all made sense. Rachel's great-grandfather, grandad, and uncles were "mountain men" living off the land, trapping the "old way," as Miss Lily would say. They made a little money on the side, or maybe even killed to put food on the table, with trapping. Their great-grandfather had probably taught them how to lay snares.

But the steel-jaw leghold traps they'd found in the old Keenan barn were so much easier to set and kill with, never mind how much pain and misery they inflicted on the animals. Dunk, Shawn, and Rachel had probably taken them and were killing on their own.

The mink trap Ashley and I had stumbled across

had probably been set by either Rachel's uncles or her grandfather. But the old rusted steel-jaw legholds —they were probably the work of Rachel, Dunk, and Shawn.

That had to be it. I knew it. Ashley knew it. Now all we had to do was go and prove it.

The best way was to catch them in the act. But it wouldn't be easy. Not at all. We'd have to hunt the hunters, basically.

I figured they'd check the traps first thing in the morning, to see what they'd caught during the night. So Ashley and I decided to get up before dawn and see if we could track them to one of the closer traps that they checked regularly.

I thought I could do it. Because, instead of looking for deer or raccoon or fox tracks, we were looking for human tracks. The tracks of Rachel's bare feet.

I was up by 4:30 in the morning. I hadn't been able to sleep much, and I was downstairs as the sky began to turn from black to a hazy gray.

When it was finally light enough to see by, I hurried upstairs into Mom's bedroom. I leaned over and gave her a kiss. "I'm goin' over to Ashley's," I whispered.

"What time is it?" she asked sleepily.

"Sun's comin' up," I whispered back.

"Be careful," she mumbled, and turned over.

"I will," I promised, and hurried away.

At the bottom of the hill, Ashley was waiting for me on her bike. I didn't say anything. She just started pedaling furiously, and I was close behind.

It was a few miles to the edge of Jupiter and the road that led to the old Keenan farm. We hadn't seen

151

anyone stirring the whole time. It was still pretty dark. You could only just make out the outlines of houses and trees in the dim light.

They'd been setting the traps over a pretty wide area. The bear trap Mark and I had come across was probably at the extreme outer edge of where they'd been laying traps. It had probably taken them days or even weeks to get it out that far.

But I figured they had to set a few close to home as well. You couldn't set all of them miles apart. It would take too long to check all of them.

There was a point not too far from the old Keenan farm where, according to one of the topography maps I'd borrowed from Mark, several streams converged to form a creek bottom. It was a perfect, natural place for animals to gather.

And a perfect place for a trap or two. Ashley and I decided to go there first and start tracking.

The creek bottom was about half a mile from the Keenan place. We ditched our bikes in some tall grass and worked our way through the wet undergrowth until we'd gotten to the point where the streams began to converge.

It was eerie walking through the forest before the sun had come up. There were sounds everywhere—birds, crickets, frogs. But you couldn't really see anything. It was all a hazy gray.

The sun still had not come up when we arrived. But by now our eyes had adjusted.

I started looking alongside the stream as we walked. Like always, I worked my way out from the stream's edge, looking for tracks. I quickly spotted all kinds of tracks, from opossum to deer. But not human tracks.

We searched for close to twenty minutes before I finally spotted the tracks. They were small and dainty and old. Maybe two or three days. But they were definitely, unmistakably the tracks of a human being, walking lightly without shoes. Just as Rachel would walk.

"Found 'em," I called out softly to Ashley.

She hurried over and knelt beside me. She could see them, too. From that point, she helped me track them downstream until we hit pay dirt.

The trap wasn't too well concealed. It was sort of jammed under an old rotten log just beside the point where the streams all fed into the creek bottom. It was a good location for the trap, but poorly laid. I doubted they'd ever catch much with it.

Ashley and I climbed a tree nearby and waited. It seemed hopeless, but I still wasn't sure that there was any other way to go about this. We just had to hope that we'd get lucky and that this was the day Rachel checked the trap.

The minutes began to drag. We waited as it began to grow lighter. The minutes began to drag even more. And still we waited.

I'd just about given up when we heard the *crack* of a twig. I glanced at Ashley. She'd heard it, too. She held up a finger to be quiet. I nodded.

An instant later, we saw the shadowy form of someone working his way quickly and clumsily through the forest. Whoever it was didn't seem to care much whether anyone heard or saw him.

The person kept tramping through the undergrowth. Ashley and I peered through the leaves from our hiding place in the tree. A few more moments and we'd be able to see the person.

She stopped beside the old rotten log and looked up for a moment. It was Rachel. I could see her clear as day. And she was checking the trap.

"Stupid idiots," we heard her mutter. She reached down and pulled the trap out a little bit, so it wasn't so concealed by the log. I'd been right. The trap had probably been set by Shawn or Dunk, and it had been set badly.

I didn't know what to do now. We'd found our hunter. But what could we do about it? We still had no proof, not really. All we'd seen was Rachel checking the trap. She could say she stumbled on it during a walk through the woods. And it wasn't like it was against the law, anyway, unless they could prove she'd stolen them from the old Keenan place.

As Rachel began to walk off, Ashley and I made a quick decision.

"Let's follow her," I whispered in her ear.

She nodded and, once Rachel was a short distance away, we clambered down the tree as silently as we could manage. We were on her trail a minute later.

It actually wasn't too hard to follow Rachel. She just tramped along through the woods, probably like she'd been doing from the moment she was born out here in the woods with all of her kin. She didn't seem to care too much about who heard her, probably because she figured there wasn't anybody up at this hour.

We made sure we were always about fifty feet behind her. We didn't want her seeing us, so we moved quickly from tree to tree as we kept up with her.

Rachel covered the ground fast. She knew her way around in the woods, probably by instinct. She just crashed through the undergrowth, which made it all that much easier for us to follow her.

She checked another trap along the way and came up empty. It was yet another trap that had not been set or concealed all that well, beside the stream in the creek bottom.

It was too bad, in a way, that there hadn't been an animal in the trap. That would have given us our proof, once she'd taken the animal from the trap.

Rachel turned from that point and began to head toward the low mountain foothills. We began to climb a little as we walked.

I figured Rachel had just enough time to check one more trap before it got too light to check them safely. Rachel was starting to trudge along as well, which told me she was tiring.

As we neared a rock outcropping of some sort, Rachel began to slow. I could hear a faint gurgling above us, probably from a spring of some sort. They'd probably laid the trap near the spring, I figured.

The woods were starting to open up more here, with the undergrowth not as thick. So Ashley and I had to hang back even farther to make sure Rachel didn't see us. We were probably a hundred and fifty yards away. But we still had a clear view of Rachel.

She scrabbled up a slope and then worked her way across it until she'd gotten to a kind of plateau. The trap was obviously set there, because she stopped, placed her hands on her hips, and let loose with a long curse.

Her voice echoed loudly in all directions. A few birds scattered. I almost felt sorry for her. She'd gotten up before dawn to check three traps, and all three had come up empty.

Rachel didn't spend time dwelling on her failure, though. She began to work her way up the slope again, undoubtedly to get to the top where she could more easily work her way back down the other side.

It was the strangest thing. As I watched Rachel turn to leave, it was almost as if time began to slow. My head cleared, and I felt like I could see for miles. Everything came into sharp focus.

As Rachel neared the crest, I saw her rear up and yell with fright. Rock shards flew off and tumbled down below. She lost her balance and fell backward, head over heels, down the slope she'd just scrabbled up.

An instant later, the largest wildcat I'd ever seen came loping up over the top of the crest. It paused only for a second before it followed Rachel.

Rachel tumbled headlong. She skidded through the undergrowth and landed with a *whomp* near where she'd been checking the trap.

There was a loud *snap* that both Ashley and I could hear distinctly, even from this distance. We both knew right away what had happened.

Rachel's loud, blood-curdling scream of terror and fright confirmed it. She'd landed on the trap, and it had sprung.

The bobcat was on her almost immediately. Rachel kept screaming, and we could hear the bobcat hissing loudly as it entered the fray.

I knew that bobcats didn't hunt people. But they would attack animals much larger than themselves if provoked. They'd been known to take on bears or cougars when cornered.

And the bobcat was probably every bit as scared right now as Rachel was. The whole thing had happened so fast, it probably reacted instinctively and attacked out of panic.

"We gotta help!" I yelled, leaping to my feet. Ashley jumped up. We both began to sprint toward the slope.

I got there a few feet ahead of Ashley and began to scramble up as fast as I could. I had no idea what I'd do once I got there, but it didn't seem to matter. I was moving on instinct now, too.

The bobcat was ripping and tearing at Rachel when I arrived a moment later. It ducked in and out, biting and clawing at Rachel, who was screaming and crying hysterically and trying to defend herself by swatting at the bobcat whenever it got close.

I could see that one of her legs had fallen squarely on the trap. The trap had sprung, catching her leg, and maybe breaking it.

The bobcat was in such a fury it didn't see me. It was intent on killing Rachel—or giving its best shot —and it wasn't about to be distracted.

I knew I had to jolt it. The bobcat's brain had gone into overdrive. It was operating on pure instinct now. It had a hurt, terrified victim pinned in a trap that had been set for it, and it was attacking with a blindness that came from hundreds of years of genetic development.

I had to upset that. I had to do something that would take the bobcat from its path of destruction.

There was only one thing to do. Rachel was screaming so loudly I knew my own voice would sound pitiful in comparison. And I couldn't throw anything, because the bobcat was much too close to Rachel and was ripping and tearing too furiously to be distracted.

I made my decision just as Ashley arrived at the top of the rocky ledge. Almost without thinking, and with time for just a short, desperate prayer to God, I rushed in.

Unlike the sleek housecat, bobcats have tufts of hair sprouting on either side of their ears. I aimed for those. I came in from behind. I knew I'd have just one chance before I too was caught in this attack.

I timed my rush so that I would arrive just as the bobcat was lunging. The bobcat leaped at Rachel, feebly trying to fend it off, and lowered its head as it bore in. I ran up from behind a moment later.

A brief, shuddering wave of adrenaline surged through me. I reached out and grabbed for both tufts of hair on either side of the bobcat's head. Both hands found their mark, and I held on for all I was worth.

I rolled backward, still holding the bobcat, and pulled with all my strength. The bobcat came free of Rachel. I heaved as hard as I could, sending the bobcat hurtling backward over my head.

The bobcat did a high, arching flip, its claws extended, its wiry frame turning desperately as all cats will do, to get its feet down before landing. The wildcat barely managed to get two of its feet righted before it landed hard and rolled.

I scrambled to my feet. The bobcat came up hissing and fighting mad. But I was between it and its victim. There were now two of us, and I wasn't caught in a trap.

I could hear Rachel moaning and whimpering with pain behind me. But I didn't turn to look. I kept my eyes riveted on the bobcat.

The smallish cat was still fighting mad. But it didn't charge. Its hair was standing straight up, and I could see the wild fury in its eyes.

It took just a fraction of a second for the secretive, wily bobcat to make up its mind. The fight had changed. It was time to move on. I gestured once with my right hand, and the bobcat reacted by turning on its heels and fleeing over the top of the slope. It was gone in a flash.

Ashley arrived at my side. Together, we turned to see what had happened to Rachel.

She was a pitiful sight. Her hair was matted from the fight. There were scratch, claw, and bite marks on her body, but not too much blood. She had collapsed in a heap soon after the bobcat had run off.

Her leg had been caught squarely in the trap she'd set. It had clamped down tight, snapping on her ankle.

I knelt down. Ashley held Rachel's head gingerly while I released the trap. Rachel whimpered only slightly as I pulled the trap free.

Her foot and ankle remained limp, and at a slightly odd angle. I was sure it was broken. But time would heal this, I knew. Once we could get her to the hospital, she'd be all right.

Ashley and I worked together to pick her up. We linked hands so we could carry her more easily. It would be a tough walk down the slope and back to Jupiter carrying Rachel, but I knew we could do it. The hard part was over now.

I glanced down at the released trap. Bits of rust had flaked off on the ground, but I could still see the ornate Surelock trademark and curlicues even from where I stood.

"Time to go, Rachel," I said softly. "Be brave. We're going to take care of you. Everything will be all right."

Rachel nodded, and then buried her face in my shoulder, crying softly. She was a far cry from the girl who'd so recently sent her German shepherd after me. A far cry.

Just before we set off, I gave the old rusted Surelock steel-jaw trap a vicious kick. I sent it careening down the rocky slope. It hit once, hard, and shattered on impact, with parts flying off in different directions.

I nodded once with satisfaction, and then turned back to the task at hand. It was time to get Rachel safely to the hospital.

About the Author

Jeff Nesbit is the author of many books for children and teenagers, including *A War of Words*, *The Sioux Society*, and *The Great Nothing Strikes Back*. He lives with his wife and their three children in Virginia.